PEN PALS:
BOOK SIX

AMY'S SONG

by Sharon Dennis Wyeth

A YEARLING BOOK

For Leslie, Robin, and Kathy

Published by
Dell Publishing
a division of
Bantam Doubleday Dell Publishing Group, Inc.
666 Fifth Avenue
New York, New York 10103

Illustrations by Wendy Wax

ISBN: 0-440-40260-3
Published by arrangement with Parachute Press, Inc.
Printed in the United States of America
January 1990
10 9 8 7 6 5 4 3 2 1
OPM

CHAPTER ONE

Dear Amy,

How would you feel if you woke up one morning and someone had suddenly changed your name from Amy to Albert? I bet you'd feel pretty bad. Not only is Albert probably not your number-one name choice, it also happens to be a boy's name. And you're a girl, right? *WELL, THAT IS HOW I FELT WHEN YOU CHANGED THE WORDS TO MY SONG!* When we decided to write songs together, I thought we made a deal that I would be the one to write the words and you would write the tune for them. But now you've changed everything. I think it is very conceited of you, and I think you owe me an apology. Until then . . .

Your pen pal,
John Adams

P.S. I have run this past the other Unknowns, and they agree with me. You Alma Stephens girls are a little too intellectual, especially you four Foxes of the Third Dimension. Maybe instead of changing the words to other

*people's songs, you should spend more time getting your
act together.*

"Come in quick!" hissed Lisa, yanking Shanon Davis
through the door by the elbow. "We have to have a
meeting. It's an emergency!"

"What now?" Shanon sighed, her arms full of books. In
Suite 3-D of Fox Hall, there seemed to be an emergency
every week! And most of them involved her dark-haired
roommate, Lisa McGreevy.

"Are you and Rob having problems again?" Shanon
asked, setting her books on the desk in the corner.

"It's not me and Rob this time," Lisa declared.

Tall, blond Palmer Durand, the third member of the
suite, stretched up from her spot on the loveseat. She was
already dressed for bed in a pale blue nightgown that was
an almost perfect match for her eyes. "This time it's Amy
and her pen pal John," she said lazily. "He sent her a really
mean letter."

Lisa pointed to one of the suite's two bedrooms. "She's
in there now, having a pillow fight!"

Shanon's hazel eyes widened. "A pillow fight with
whom?"

Palmer shrugged. "With John, of course."

Shanon drew in a breath. From the other side of the
closed bedroom door, Amy Ho's angry voice could be
clearly heard.

"You mean John Adams is here at Alma Stephens?"
Shanon squeaked. "Without permission at eight-thirty on
a Monday night? We're not even supposed to see boys in

2

the common room! Not even on weekends! If somebody finds out about this—"

"Calm down," Lisa broke in. "Of course John isn't *really* here. Amy's just pretending. She's in there punching out a pillow."

Shanon sunk down onto the couch next to Palmer. "Oh, that kind of pillow fight," she said in relief. Lisa had thought up the tactic a few weeks ago after Kate Majors, the dorm monitor, had caught her raiding the refrigerator. Lisa had bitten her tongue and remained quiet throughout the older girl's long, officious lecture, but it hadn't been easy. And the minute she was safe in Suite 3-D, she'd pretended her pillow was Kate and told her off loud and clear. Now, Amy was in the next room telling John just what she thought of him.

"How long has Amy been at it?" Shanon asked.

"For the past ten minutes," Lisa replied, rolling her big, brown eyes dramatically.

"She was actually yelling in Chinese," Palmer reported. "At least I assume that's what it was."

"Amy knows a few Chinese words from her grandmother," chuckled Shanon. She tiptoed across the room and put her ear to the bedroom door.

As Shanon turned back toward the sitting room, the door swung open and Amy Ho stood there, dressed in a black jersey jumpsuit. Her spiked black hair seemed to be sticking up more than usual.

"Feel better?" Lisa asked.

"I heard about John's letter," Shanon said sympathetically.

3

"Wait until you read it," Amy muttered, tossing the note over. "He called me conceited! But I think he's really arrogant!"

Palmer smiled slyly. "Well, how come you keep him as a pen pal?"

"Because! Because we get along together," Amy sputtered. "Well, we always did—until this disagreement."

"This kind of thing can be bad for the rest of us," said Lisa. "Don't forget that John lives with Rob and Mars. If you and he have a fight, it might affect things for Shanon and me with our pen pals."

"Don't *say* that!" Shanon cried. "Mars and I get along great."

"So do Rob and I," said Lisa firmly.

"Sam O'Leary and I are fine, too," Palmer added with a sigh. "For once I'm glad he goes to Brighton High instead of Ardsley. So if John and Mars and Rob decide to drop you three, it wouldn't affect me."

"I wouldn't be so sure about that," Lisa said, lifting a dark eyebrow. "Don't forget that Sam used to go to Ardsley, too, and he and Mars are friends. If the Unknowns start having a bad opinion of us Foxes, more than likely Sam will hear about it."

"Ummm, I see what you mean," Palmer grumbled.

"That's silly," Amy protested. "Just because John and I are having a fight, that doesn't mean your pen pals will get angry at you. Lisa and Rob have had their own disagreements," she reminded them.

"Not like this," Lisa insisted. "John's already told our pen pals about the problem he was having with you. And he said the Foxes of the Third Dimension should get our act together—that means all of us!"

Amy thought for a moment. "John shouldn't have done that. He shouldn't have gotten you guys involved in our fight."

"But he has," Lisa said.

Amy sat down on the floor cross-legged. The pillow fight had made her feel calmer, but she still didn't see what John was so upset about. He wasn't usually so touchy. And why bring the other Foxes into their argument? When Lisa had first thought up the idea of advertising in the Ardsley Academy newspaper for boy pen pals, Shanon and Palmer hadn't been very enthusiastic. But Amy had thought it was a great idea. It had seemed the perfect way for the residents of the all-girl Alma Stephens boarding school to meet students from Ardsley Academy, the nearby boys' school. But now she wasn't so sure.

Lisa grabbed a bag of popcorn off the bookshelf. "I think this calls for an official meeting of the Foxes of the Third Dimension." Foxes of the Third Dimension was the code name the girls had thought of for their pen pal advertisement. The suite at Ardsley where Amy's, Shanon's, and Lisa's pen pals lived had a code name, too: The Unknown. There'd been a fourth Unknown—Simmie Randolph—but he and Palmer had had a falling out and now she was happily corresponding with Sam O'Leary.

"Good idea," said Amy, falling onto her stomach and doing a push-up. "I could use some advice on how to handle this. John and I agreed to write a song together. I wouldn't have changed his words unless I thought they needed improvement. Anyway, the song sounds much better now!"

"Too bad John doesn't think so," Lisa said dryly.

"I know what!" Shanon said, kicking off her loafers. "Amy, why don't you sing us both versions? That way we can decide which one is better—yours or John's."

"Good idea," Lisa agreed. "Only it doesn't matter in the long run which song is better. Amy still has to apologize."

"Absolutely," Palmer said, giving her long legs a stretch. "Do you mind if we have the meeting in our room? I want to give myself a mini-facial before lights out."

The four Foxes crowded into the room shared by Amy and Palmer. While Amy settled onto her own bed beneath a gigantic Joan Jett poster, Shanon and Lisa perched on Palmer's frilly white bedspread. Taking a position in front of the mirror, Palmer started smearing green stuff all over her perfect pink skin.

"The meeting of the Foxes of the Third Dimension is now called to order," Lisa announced.

Tossing her sandy-brown braid over one shoulder, Shanon reached into the popcorn bag. She usually took a back seat when it came to meetings, since Lisa was so good at running things.

"Okay," said Amy. "Since the meeting's about me, here's the story. But first maybe you'd better get a load of John Adams' letter."

"We've already seen that," Palmer mumbled through her face mask.

"No, you haven't," said Amy. "This is the one he sent

6

me a couple of weeks ago, with the words to his song." She passed around a piece of paper with bold blue writing on it.

Lisa examined the letter.

"Let me see it," Palmer demanded as Lisa grabbed a handful of popcorn.

Dear Amy,

I am glad we are collaborating on a new song. Here are the words I came up with for the melody you sent me on the cassette tape. I hope you like them. The name of the song is "The Ballad of Young Willie the Poet."

> *I was standing in the mist*
> *When I thought I heard a hiss.*
> *It was a man all dressed in regal garb.*
> *He turned and caught my eye.*
> *I said oh me, oh my.*
> *I know you, you are young Willie the Poet.*
> *Yes I am, said he. I go down in his-to-ry.*
> *I am a writer of romantic ver-se.*
> *I don't rehear-se—*

"Stop!" squawked Palmer. "That's boring."

"Maybe it sounds better with Amy's music," Shanon said hopefully.

Amy shook her head. "It doesn't. That's why I made the changes."

"What kind of changes did you make?" Lisa asked, slipping the polka dot tie off her ponytail and grabbing a hairbrush.

Amy shrugged. "Nothing too major, just the sex of it."

"The what?" Shanon blushed.

Palmer giggled.

"Explain, puh-lease!" Lisa demanded.

"I changed the sex of the main character in the song," Amy said. "John wrote about this dweeby young poet named Willie. I kept a lot of his words, but I changed it to a song about a beautiful old lady named Willameena."

"Oh, my gosh!" Lisa laughed. "No wonder John's so mad!"

Palmer giggled again. "Changing the sex of a song is very serious!"

"I don't think that's so terrible," Shanon put in. "It's still the same song, isn't it?"

"Well, actually," Amy said sheepishly, "I changed a couple of other things, too—like the word poet. I changed that to bard, because it rhymed better. And then I—"

"Play it for us," Shanon suggested.

Amy's eyes lit up and she grabbed her guitar. "I think you'll agree it's a lot better now," she said, strumming softly. "And a lot of the verse is still the same."

Palmer yawned. "Then skip to the chorus."

Amy smiled and began to sing. Her voice, which was low for a girl, was full of humor.

> "It's Willa, Willameena the Bard.
> Let me give you my card.
> Yeah, it's written down in po-e-try!
> ROCK OUT, WILLA—"

8

There was an angry thump on the ceiling.

"Uh-oh! I guess John's not the only one who doesn't like my song," Amy said, putting her guitar down.

"Must be Kate Majors," Lisa grumbled.

"What a pain that girl is," Palmer said, pouting.

"It's not Kate," said Shanon, listening for another thump. "It came from upstairs. It must be Brenda. She broke her toe last week. She probably needs to rest. Maybe she made that thump with one of her crutches."

"Whoever it is," huffed Palmer, "it is not too late for singing!"

There was a loud knocking, this time at the sitting-room door. "Lights out in there!" a high voice called with authority.

"Now, *that* was Kate," Shanon whispered as Lisa hit the light switch on the wall. Palmer and Amy immediately turned on some flashlights.

"Should we go on with the meeting?" Lisa whispered through the half-darkness.

"Yes. But I don't think I'd better sing anymore," Amy said. "I already have two demerits for that time we got caught raiding the kitchen."

The four girls were silent.

"We've got to come to a decision," Lisa insisted, keeping her voice down. Palmer and Amy shone their lights on her. "I say that no matter how great your song is, Amy, you should apologize to John."

Amy looked sullen. "But it's so much better my way."

"You and John made a deal," Shanon reminded her.

9

"And artists are very sensitive. That's probably why he sent you such an angry letter."

"Yes, you should definitely say you're sorry," chimed in Palmer, "especially since John might be talking to Sam O'Leary. I wouldn't want Sam getting the wrong idea about us—John said we're 'too intellectual,' remember?"

"Okay," Amy said flatly. "You win. I'll apologize."

Lisa jumped up and scurried to the corner. Shining the flashlight on the desk, she rummaged through the top drawer.

"What are you looking for?" asked Palmer.

"This," Lisa said, grabbing some stationery. "If we're going to send some letters to our pen pals tomorrow . . . tonight we've got to write!"

CHAPTER TWO

———◆———

Dear Rob,

This is a late-night letter. In fact, it is on the stroke of midnight and I think I am the last one up, though I can't tell what's going on in Amy and Palmer's room. I am sure that Shanon is asleep because she is completely buried under the covers. How do you like to sleep, with the covers on or off? I like the covers off and the window open, but Shanon is always cold, so it can only be opened a crack. Back home at my parents' house in Pennsylvania, we never had the thermostat above sixty degrees in winter. Every Christmas my mother bought me and my brother Reggie this horrible long underwear! Anyway, I guess I just got used to being cold all the time, so now I like it—especially when I'm sleeping. Not that I sleep much. I have insomnia. When people like Shanon are winding down, my mind is just getting started. I keep her awake as long as I can, but she usually conks out on me by ten thirty. Of course it doesn't help that the only light we can have after nine thirty is the flashlight. Anyway, being up at night is

11

interesting. When I was little, I did all kinds of things. I used to get up and play with my toys, and once—when I had actually fallen asleep, get this!—my mom caught me sleepwalking. I was going to the refrigerator to get an ice pop. When I told the other Foxes that I used to walk in my sleep, Palmer got scared. She thought I might get up at night and come into her room. Isn't that stupid? It's true that sometimes Palmer is so obnoxious that I feel like strangling her, ha-ha, but I wouldn't do it while I was sleepwalking.

If you're wondering why I've stayed up so late to write to you instead of waiting until the morning, it's because we got (rather, Amy got) this letter from John in which he was very angry. He said that the other Unknowns agreed with him. I'm writing to say that I hope you aren't mad at me just because John is mad at Amy. It would be silly for the other Unknowns and Sam to be mad at us for something Amy did. Not that we are not loyal to Amy. After all, she is one of the Foxes.

We are going on a class trip soon, but we don't know where. Miss Pryn and the administration haven't announced it yet. Last year's freshman class went to the Rockies. It was supposedly beautiful, but it was still out in the boonies. I guess they wouldn't ever think of taking a class trip to a city. Brenda Smith, this fourth-form girl who lives upstairs and has broken her toe, says it's because there are too many PG movies available there. As you know, movies are one of my fav raves. Do you know that we have only one television in Fox Hall? And the VCR is broken, which means that we can't even see movies that way.

It's been such a long time since you and I have seen each other. I remember what you look like, though, because I have your picture. It's good to see somebody's face in your mind when you are writing to them. I guess while I'm writing this letter, you're probably asleep. I'm sitting on the floor under our window right now. I have on a pair of black bike pants with an orange stripe. I'm also wearing a black tank top. Of course I should be in my pajamas, but maybe I'll sleep in my clothes. Since we always have to wear skirts and blouses to class, there are only a few hours a day when we get to look normal. By the way, I'm also wearing your class pin. It's pinned to my black tank top. It's on the left side, next to my heart, which is where I always pin it. I hope to see you again sometime in the future. Please write me a letter.

Your pen pal,
Lisa

P.S. I think I told you that my brother Reggie has this new girlfriend from Alma who I can't stand. Her name is Kate Majors and she's too bossy and quite a dweeb. Could you find out if Reggie really likes her? You must run into him sometimes, since you both go to Ardsley. I would appreciate it. By the way, Amy is sending an apology to John.

Dear Mars,

Lisa said I have to write to you before I go to bed. Please use your influence with John to make him forgive Amy.

She is writing to him herself, and I'm sure she'll write a very good apology. I don't think she meant any harm by changing his song lyrics. I suppose I can identify with how upset John was about this. When I wrote my story in The Alma Ledger *about what Alma Stephens had in common with other girls' boarding schools, the editor of the paper, Dolores Countee, changed a lot of it around. And that was hard to swallow. Now my friend Kate edits most of my stories and she is very good about making changes.*

We are going on a class trip soon, and I am very excited. I can't wait to find out where it is. I hope it's someplace historical like Williamsburg, Virginia. I've always wanted to go there. My parents were never too big on vacations, so there are lots of places I'd like to see.

How are you doing in your subjects? Is Spanish still your favorite? English is still mine. Mr. Griffith is the best teacher in the whole world. He just told us about a short story contest. I think I might enter it.

Excuse my handwriting. My eyes are closing and I am falling asleep.

Your pen pal,
Shanon

P.S. John said he thinks Alma girls are too intellectual. I hope you don't think that.

Dear Sam,

Thank you for the friendly letter you sent me. Guess what? I saw an ad for Suzy's Shoe Emporium in The Ledger! *Are you still working there on weekends? How are things going with your band, Sam and the Fantasy? I hope*

14

you get some engagements sometime soon where I can hear you, maybe at Alma Stephens. I don't have much to write, except that if you happen to talk to John Adams, Amy's Ardie pen pal, I had nothing to do with anything. They had a major argument over a song. Isn't that silly? I'm sure it will not affect anything between me and you, though. Does your school have dances like Ardsley Academy does? Looking forward to your next letter.

Your pen pal,
Palmer Durand

P.S. Do you play tennis?

Dear John,

If I hurt your feelings, I apologize. Shanon says it must be because you are sensitive. I have an idea. The next time we get together, why don't we play the two versions of our song and see which one is better? I really love "Willameena" and I cannot give up my words just because you don't want the song to be about a woman. It would be like murdering someone. I hope we can still be friends. And, like I said, I apologize. But I will not change the words to my song because I think they are better. And making the song the best way you know how is what is most important.

Yours truly,
Amy

CHAPTER THREE

Dear Lisa,

Your letter was so long. You must have had writer's
cramp by the time you finished it. I am a night owl, too. I
will do anything to stay awake. Mars and John don't like
to tolerate it. Arthur (or, as you girls call him, Mars) must
have his zzzs just like your roommate Shanon. Guess they
are a good match for pen pals, ha-ha! But I am like you. I
like life in the fast lane.

Don't worry—John may be down on Alma because of
Amy, but far be it from me to accuse anyone of being too
intellectual. Their song is their own business and has
nothing to do with you and me being pen pals. Confidentially, I think John's stuff is pretty drippy at times, though
this "Young Willie" isn't bad. I'm sure Amy's song is good,
too.

Do you still have on your black tank top? Thinking
about you wearing my pin over your heart makes me feel
great. Sorry I have to go now. Randolph and I have a
handball game. He sometimes asks about Palmer, but I

don't say anything. It was rude of her to dump him, but I suppose it was necessary. I hope the same thing doesn't happen to your suitemate Amy, since John is still rather mad. He is a straight dude but has the soul of an artist.

Love,
Rob

P.S. *Here's a new pic of me. I thought you might need an update.*

P.P.S. *I tried to check out your brother for you, but we don't seem to speak the same language. Does he have a problem talking? When I say "Hi" to him or ask him a question, he just blinks at me and never answers. I hate to say it, but he is a true dweeb. Maybe he and this girl at your school are just right for each other.*

Dear Shanon,

One of the reasons I enjoy getting your letters is that I have always thought of you as more intellectual and smarter than I am. So if John says that Alma girls are intellectual, it is not going to influence me in any way. I haven't got much news except that he is still mad at Amy. I think she has shattered his ego. The guy hates criticism.

As for myself, I have recently decorated my room. Before it was empty. But I found an old cuckoo clock in a junk shop in town. I fixed it and it works. Rob finds it annoying, which makes it even funnier. I love ribbing the guy. Is that school of yours ever going to throw another party? I'd like to see you again so I can pull your pigtail. Yes, Spanish is still my favorite subject.

Back to the subject of John—if you want to know the truth, I think he has a gigantic crush on Amy Ho. That's

17

why he got so mad when she didn't completely like the stuff he wrote.

Adios,
Mars

Dear Palmer,

Yes, I am still working there on the weekends. Just waiting around for another visit from Cinderella. Excuse the joke, but I'll never forget the funny way we met that time when you and your roommates were in town together and I was selling shoes at the store.

To answer your other question, The Fantasy is doing fine. I practice with the band after school every evening, which drives my family nuts. The band's sound is good, but we have two problems—new material and new gigs. I'm sure something will turn up. Hope you are doing okay with your schoolwork and everything else. Sorry to disappoint you, but I thought I told you I don't play tennis.

Sincerely,
Sam O'Leary

P.S. I have not spoken to John, but I do not agree with you that songs are silly. They are sacred. In any case, I would never have an opinion about you or anything else just because John or someone told me to have it. I have my own opinions.

Dear Amy,

If you will not change the song, forget having me as a collaborator. It's either me or "Willameena."

John Adams

P.S. I do not accept your apology, because it wasn't one.

18

CHAPTER FOUR

"But soft! What light through yonder window breaks? . . ."

Mr. Griffith looked up at his third-form English class before continuing.

"Isn't his voice heavenly?" Lisa whispered to Shanon.

"He's great," Shanon breathed back, her eyes riveted on the handsome English teacher. "Especially when he reads from *Romeo and Juliet*."

". . . See how she leans her cheek upon her hand!/O that I were a glove upon that hand/That I might touch that cheek."

Dan Griffith closed his book of Shakespearean plays, placed it on his desk, and looked around the room expectantly. Lisa and Shanon sat in the front row staring. Shanon was thinking how lucky they were to have an English teacher with such beautiful green eyes plus such a beautiful reading voice and how romantic it must be for Miss Grayson. Maggie Grayson was the girls' French teacher and also the faculty advisor for Fox Hall. Shanon

19

was absolutely certain that the two attractive young teachers were dating each other.

Lisa was also sure Mr. Griffith and Miss Grayson were having a romance, but at the moment her mind was on Romeo. If Shakespeare's hero were alive today, what would he look like? she wondered. Probably like Rob, Lisa thought wistfully, tall with dark curly hair. Of course, Romeo's voice would probably be more like Mr. Griffith's. Rob's voice had still been changing the last time Lisa saw him. Sometimes it was deep like Mr. Griffith's, but sometimes it cracked.

On the other side of the room, Amy was sitting next to Muffin Talbot. Muffin, who was the shortest person in school, had her eyes glued to her notebook. Amy, whose long metal earrings came dangerously close to violating the rule against distracting accessories, liked her teacher's deep voice, too, but she was having trouble keeping her mind on Romeo and Juliet. She had her own relationship—and her own feud—to think about.

"Well, what do you think of this scene?" Mr. Griffith quizzed them. Circling the room, he stopped at Palmer's desk. Palmer's pale blue eyes were staring dreamily out the window. The teacher tapped her gently on the shoulder. "Are you with us, Miss Durand?" he asked.

"Uh, yes sir," Palmer replied, trying to look as if she hadn't just been fantasizing about Sam and the Fantasy. "I . . . I lost my train of thought," she bluffed. "Could you repeat the question?"

"I was just wondering what you think about this speech of Romeo's."

"I guess it's okay," she replied, taking a stab at it.

20

"I guess you'd better get back on the track again," said Mr. Griffith. The popular teacher was nice, but he could be stern also. "Does anyone here have something intelligent to say about Romeo and Juliet?"

"I think the balcony scene contains some of the most romantic language Shakespeare ever wrote," Shanon volunteered.

"I agree," Lisa piped up. "If I were Juliet, I'd be swept off my feet by Romeo too. He says such neat things to her. He says she's more beautiful than the moon!"

Mr. Griffith's green eyes twinkled. "I'm glad to see that you all appreciate the work of Shakespeare." He glanced at Muffin. "And what are your impressions, Miss Talbot?"

Muffin thought for a minute. "I think they were awfully mature for teenagers."

"Good point," said Mr. Griffith. "It's hard to imagine teenagers today taking such a hand in their own destinies."

"I disagree!" Amy said hotly. "I think there are lots of girls nowadays who are quite mature for their ages. They're not at all afraid to have their opinions. It's the boys who are the immature ones!"

Mr. Griffith looked puzzled. "Are you referring to Romeo?"

Amy blushed. "Sort of," she mumbled. "I guess I'm talking about all boys."

Lisa smothered a giggle. "I guess she's talking about John," she whispered to Shanon.

"I know," Shanon whispered back. "She's still mad at him."

A soft tittering rippled through the classroom. Mr. Griffith cleared his throat. "The discussion of our

21

Shakespearean play this morning brings me to a very important announcement."

"Is it about the short story contest?" Shanon blurted out.

"No," Mr. Griffith replied. "It's about the class trip."

"The class trip!" exclaimed Lisa. "Where are we going?"

"Yes, where?" the class clamored.

Mr. Griffith held up a hand to silence them. "May we have a bit more decorum, please, ladies?" Reaching into his briefcase, he went on. "Since Miss Davis has asked about the short story contest, I'll deal with that first." He handed her an information sheet. "This will tell you all you need to know in order to submit a story," he told Shanon. "I hope that you're a brave soul. The theme is ghost stories!"

"Ooooo!" said Lisa. "Ghost stories."

Mr. Griffith shot her a look.

"The theme sounds challenging," said Shanon. "I'll do my best to write something."

Amy raised her hand. "Now will you please tell us where we're going on the class trip?"

"Very well," Mr. Griffith replied. He cracked a smile. "I have to admit I'm just as excited as I think you're going to be."

"Don't keep us in suspense," begged Palmer. "Where is it?"

The handsome teacher beamed. Then, very slowly and deliberately, he made his announcement: "Miss Grayson and I and some of the other faculty are taking the whole freshman class to . . . London! The home of William Shakespeare!"

The class burst into uncontrollable chatter.

Lisa gasped. "London! All my life I've wanted to go there!"

"I lived there for a while when I was five years old," Amy said enthusiastically. "It's incredible!"

"I hear it's a great place to shop, too," said Palmer.

"And it's so historic!" Shanon added. She was so excited she thought she might faint. "I can't believe it! I've never even been on an airplane before! And now I'm going to be flying all the way to Europe!"

Everyone in the class started talking at once. The girls wanted to know how long they'd be staying—and where.

"All your questions will be answered in due course," Mr. Griffith said over the uproar. "And now—class dismissed." He flashed them another smile. "So much for decorum."

All the way across the quad to the dining hall, the girls marveled over the trip.

"Too awesome," said Lisa. "Imagine the faculty deciding to take us to London!"

"I'm hitting the record stores as soon as I get there," Amy announced. "London is the home of some very important rock music."

"I'm stocking up on cashmere sweaters," said Palmer decisively. "My mom says that England is the only place to buy them."

Shanon gulped. "Wait a minute. . . . I just thought of something."

"What?" said Lisa.

"It must cost a fortune to go to London," said Shanon. "Who's going to pay for it? I—I hope *we're* not supposed to."

Lisa chortled. "Us? Be real. I haven't got that kind of money."

"Maybe the school is handling it," Amy said, shrugging.

"What's the difference?" said Palmer. "If we have to pay, we can just put it on our charge cards."

Shanon rolled her eyes. "Excuse me, but I don't happen to have a charge card. I don't even have a passport."

Palmer wrinkled her nose. "You don't have a *passport*? Where have you been?"

"Not jet-setting like you," Lisa jumped in. Shanon was the only one of the Foxes whose family wasn't wealthy, and Lisa didn't want her friend to feel embarrassed about it.

Amy hooked Palmer's elbow. "Everybody in the world hasn't been all over the world, princess. Come on, let's go to the dining hall."

As they headed toward the dining hall, Shanon turned to Lisa with a frown.

"Do you have your own passport?" she asked.

Lisa shrugged. "Uh-huh. My parents got me one. Don't worry. I'm sure your parents can get you one, too."

"Or maybe the school will," Amy added.

"I guess you're right," said Shanon.

"And as far as the cost is concerned," Lisa chimed in, "I bet the school will take care of that too."

"They probably have some deal with an alumna who owns an airline," Palmer reasoned.

"In any case," Lisa told Shanon, "you shouldn't worry about it. Nobody's going to send you a bill."

"Of course not," giggled Amy. "Wouldn't it be ridiculous? Sending a bill to somebody our age?"

Shanon smiled. "You're right. I always worry about everything. My scholarship must cover the cost of class trips as well as tuition!"

Lisa patted her shoulder. "I'm sure it does."

As they stood on the steps of the dining hall, Palmer sniffed and wrinkled her nose again. "What's on the lunch menu?"

"Bangers!" Lisa said hungrily.

"Great," said Amy.

"Not great," Palmer objected. "I say let's go to the snack bar. Bangers give me a pain. I'm sure there's all kinds of disgusting things inside them."

"They're only English sausages," Lisa argued. "And Mrs. Butter makes them just right. I'm sure we'll be eating loads of them on our trip to London."

"All the more reason to buy a good American hamburger at the snack bar now," Palmer nagged.

"Sorry," Shanon cut in quietly, "but if you're going to the snack bar, count me out. I can't afford it."

"Come on," Lisa said, glancing at Shanon protectively, "we're already at the dining hall, so we might as well eat here. Besides, why should we spend money for hamburgers when we can eat here for free? We should save money for our London trip." She gave the door a shove and held it open for Amy and Shanon.

"Oh, all right!" Palmer grumbled. "But I don't see what

not eating hamburgers has to do with buying cashmere sweaters," she added, following them inside.

In the lunch line, Palmer asked Mrs. Butter for some yogurt.

"Nonsense," the English cook scolded. "That stuff won't put the roses in your cheeks like these lovely sausages!"

"Have you heard?" Lisa asked cheerfully. "We're going to London!"

"Yes, dearie," Mrs. Butter said, smiling. "I wish I could go right along with you in a suitcase! I'd visit my people in Liverpool!"

"Speaking of suitcases," Palmer muttered, "I'm going to buy some new luggage. I only brought two suitcases with me to Alma."

"You won't need more than that," said Amy, grabbing a juice. "I'm sure I can fit everything I'll need in a knapsack."

"Maybe *you* can," Palmer said, as they found seats at their favorite table.

"I can hardly wait to write Rob about this," Lisa exclaimed. "He's been to lots of places. I wonder if London is one of them."

"I'm sure Sam has been there," said Palmer. "London's his kind of city."

"What makes you think that?" Amy asked, cutting into her banger.

"Just a feeling," Palmer replied, flashing a bright smile. "I really don't know that much about him yet. It's so great having a new pen pal, so mysterious! Imagine how many things there are for me to find out about Sam."

"It *is* fun," Shanon agreed. "I feel as if Mars and I are old friends already. A lot has gone on through our letters."

"A lot has gone on with my letters with John," Amy muttered, "but it hasn't been all that much fun lately."

Lisa put down her fork. "That's because you're so stubborn."

"That's not the reason," Amy countered. "It's because John doesn't like me. If he did, he would at least agree to hear my words to 'Willameena.' "

"But you made a deal," Lisa argued.

Palmer sighed. "Can't we please talk about something else! Now that we know Sam and Mars and Rob are still going to write to us no matter what happens between John and Amy"—she paused to take a breath—"I say it's really none of our business."

"Yes, let's just drop the subject," said Amy, gulping her juice. "If John doesn't like me, then I don't like him. Anyway, as far as writing songs is concerned, I have a right to my own opinions."

"But what if you found out that John does like you?" Lisa said, eyeing Shanon.

"He doesn't!" Amy insisted.

"That's not what Mars says," Shanon ventured.

Amy blushed. "Did Mars tell you something about John and me in a letter? What was it?"

"Mars said that John had a crush on you," Shanon told her.

"It's not true!" Amy said, blushing even more deeply. "How does Mars know anyway?"

"He and John are suitemates," Shanon replied. "They know everything about each other, just like we do."

Lisa's eyes shone mischievously. "That's probably why John got so mad when you changed the words to his song. He likes you so much, it drove him crazy to think you didn't like something he'd written."

Amy fluffed her hair up nervously and jiggled her foot. Then she took a piece of bubble gum out of her knapsack. She'd recently begun thinking of John Adams as more than just a friend, but she'd never dreamed he felt the same. Most of their letters were so impersonal. And the only thing they seemed to have in common was that they both liked to write songs.

"Are you sure that's true?" Amy asked cautiously.

"You can see Mars's letter for yourself," Shanon offered.

"This is *so* romantic!" Lisa said. "Who knows? John may even want to ask you to be his girlfriend!"

Amy felt a sinking feeling. "Not now," she said quietly. "He's madder at me than ever. I wrote him another letter I didn't tell you about."

"You did?" said Lisa. "What did it say?"

Amy swallowed. "Remember when he wrote to me that I should choose between him and 'Willameena'? Well, I wrote him back and said . . . I didn't choose him."

"Wow," murmured Shanon, "that's awful. Maybe you should—"

Shanon broke off in mid-sentence as Brenda Smith and Kate Majors walked over to the table. Brenda was on crutches because of her broken toe, and Kate was carrying her tray for her.

"Hi!" Kate said cheerfully.

"Hi," Lisa said, glancing away. Kate was one of her least

favorite people, but since she was Shanon's friend, Lisa had to put up with her. She just hoped her brother Reggie wasn't too serious about Kate.

"I just came back from a meeting with the Alma Social Committee," Kate announced, adjusting her glasses. "We've settled on the theme for our next dance. It's going to be the sixties."

"Wow," said Lisa, "as in the sixties when the hippies were around? Sounds like fun. When is it?"

Brenda patted her frizzy blonde hair. "Just after your class's trip. I hope my toe's okay by then. I love the songs of that era."

"Me too!" Amy agreed. "Especially The Grateful Dead!"

"As usual," Kate continued, "Ardsley has been issued a general invite."

"Can I invite a boy from Brighton High?" Palmer asked quickly.

Kate shrugged. "I don't see why not, as long as you clear it with Miss Grayson."

"Great," Palmer said, her blue eyes shining. "I'll invite my new pen pal, Sam O'Leary—of Sam and the Fantasy."

"Who?" said Brenda.

Palmer took out her wallet. "Here," she said, handing Brenda a photo of her good-looking blond pen pal.

"His hair is sort of long, isn't it?" said Kate, peering over Brenda's shoulder. "That would never go over at Ardsley."

"That's why he goes to Brighton," Palmer said blithely. "He likes the freedom. He can wear his hair any way he wants there."

29

"Interesting," Brenda said, eyeing the photo.

"I have a new picture of Rob," said Lisa. "Want to see?"

Brenda nodded, and Lisa opened her wallet. Dark-haired Rob had posed outside his dorm, Kirby Hall, wearing a red muscle shirt.

"Also cute," Brenda said approvingly.

"Here's *my* pen pal," Shanon said, shyly offering a snapshot of Mars.

Brenda giggled at the picture of Mars sticking his tongue out at the camera. "He's funny-looking."

"He *is* funny," Shanon said, blushing. "But I think he's great-looking!"

Brenda sighed. "You guys sure were smart. With this pen pal thing, you have guaranteed dates for the sixties dance."

"By the way," Kate informed them, "we're asking everyone to come in sixties-type clothing."

"This is perfect," said Lisa. "After we come back from London, there'll be something even cooler to look forward to! I have so much to tell Rob, I'll have to send two letters."

Brenda nudged Amy. "What about your pen pal? Got any new pictures of him?"

"Just the old one," Amy mumbled.

Brenda adjusted the bow in her hair. "That's okay. I remember what he looks like. He's tall and has red hair. And he wrote that song with you, 'Cabin Fever.' A lot of girls I know think he's really cool."

Amy sat up. "Like who?"

Brenda shrugged. "Like Molly Macmillan, who goes to

Brier Hall. She has a huge crush on John Adams. By the way, Brier Hall is having a dance the same night we are."

"Oh, no!" said Lisa. "That's not fair! They're probably going to invite Ardsley too."

Kate nodded. "That's what I heard."

"Uh-oh," said Palmer, "I'd better invite Sam to The Sixties right away. I wouldn't want him to get invited to Brier Hall first."

Brenda turned to Amy. "What about John? Are you going to invite him?"

Amy swallowed. "I guess so."

"They just had a fight," Palmer volunteered.

"That's okay," Shanon said sympathetically. "Amy can still invite him."

"You think so?" Amy moaned. "After that last letter, I bet he won't come. He'll probably go to Brier Hall instead."

"You'd better think of a way to apologize to John again, before it's too late!" Palmer told Amy.

Amy sighed. "It's no use. No matter what I write, he'll never forgive me."

"Call him on the phone," Palmer suggested.

Amy cringed with embarrassment. "I couldn't."

"I know!" said Lisa. "You can send him a tape—make a recording to tell him how sorry you are."

"Better still," said Shanon, "you could sing it!"

"Oh, no!" Amy cried. "I could never do that. First of all, my singing voice is not the greatest."

"That's not true!" Lisa protested. "You're improving."

Amy glanced at Palmer. "What do you think?"

31

"I guess your voice is improving," she said with a shrug. "Anyway, it's not the voice that counts, it's the words."

"True," said Amy. "But what am I going to sing to John—that I'm sorry?"

"No," said Shanon. "Just sing the song you wrote together, but with John's words! Then he'll know your apology is really sincere."

"What a great idea!" Lisa cried. "Sing 'Young Willie.'"

Amy giggled. "It *is* sort of an unusual way of apologizing. . . ."

"Give it a try," Brenda encouraged. "I think you're really lucky to have a pen pal like John Adams."

Amy grinned. "I *will* try it," she said. She thought she was lucky to have John as a pen pal, too, especially now that she knew he liked her. To think she'd almost ruined everything—and all because of a silly song.

CHAPTER FIVE

Dear Rob,

If you think I got writer's cramp the last time I wrote, wait until you read this letter. Except tonight I may not be able to spend too much time writing to you because tomorrow we have a test in Latin, and Miss Dewar gave me a C minus on my last quiz. Who cares if the word for "horse" in Latin is equus? *Does anybody go around talking about equus-back riding? Do people on dude ranches saddle up their equuses? My point is that Latin is a dead language, so why should we study it? Shanon says that Latin is the root of everything, and she actually likes to read stuff in it about the ancient Romans in her spare time. I really like my roommate, but sometimes I don't understand her.*

To get to the true point of this letter, we are going to London! Are you ready for this? Miss Pryn and the faculty have decided to fly the whole third-form class there! For eight days. I can't wait, needless to say. It will be so great to have a change. One whole entire week of no classes! Not only that, but we'll be in the city for a change. If I have anything to say about it, I'll be going to a different movie every single night. Isn't it neat of Alma to send us on such a great vacation? Where do you Ardies go on your class trips? We will not be leaving for a while, so I'll write you again before I go, and of course I'll send you a postcard from London.

The other thing I have to say is that as you can see from the enclosed invitation, there is a dance as soon as we come back, on the 29th of next month. I know it's far away, but we have to plan ahead with the trip coming up. It's eleven

34

o'clock now and I am using my flashlight to finish this. I still haven't gone over the Latin vocabulary. I'm wearing a denim jumpsuit and some hoop earrings and your pin. Good night for now. Or maybe, since I'll soon be in London, I should sign off by saying—

Cheerio!
Lisa

Dear Lisa,

I got the invitation. Your artwork is incredible. So far I have nothing on for that Saturday. You certainly are asking far in advance. Did you hear that Brier Hall is also giving a dance that night? The Unknown and I were thinking about going to that, but now that The Sixties has come up, we'll be at Alma. Sounds neat. My dad grew up in the sixties and had really long hair. Maybe I'll write him for research. I'd grow my hair, but you know how it is over here at the penitentiary. The last guy who tried that got trimmed by the headmaster's personal barber. Hey, the London trip sounds excellent. What's going on? Is Alma suddenly becoming progressive? I can just see you and Amy Ho let loose in London now. To answer your question, I've never been there. I sure would like to go, though. The place has a reputation as a wild city—home of the punk rockers. I'm really happy for you, but I will miss you. England is a thousand miles away from Ardsley Academy.

Love,
Rob

P.S. I am wearing blue jeans. Here is another picture of me so you won't forget.

Dear Rob,

    Thanks for the picture. There is no way in the world, even if we were thousands of miles apart, that I would ever forget you.

Love,
Lisa

Dear Mars,

    Something very nice has happened. Our class is going to England. I thought I was lucky when I got into Alma Stephens with a scholarship, but I never dreamed that when I came here I would also get my first trip on an airplane. Even my mother has not been on a plane before. Have you ever flown? Is it scary? Have you been to England? You will also see from the invitation I am enclosing (Lisa drew it) that we are having a dance. I hope that you can come. It will be great to see you. Another exciting thing that's happened is that I have decided to enter a short story contest. The theme of the contest is ghost stories! I don't know much about ghosts, but I'm going to try my hand at it. And speaking of writing . . . write back soon!

Your friend,
Shanon

Dear Shanon babe,

    You are too sweet. I mean your letters are so nice. I also

like the "groovy" invitation! As you can see, I am practicing up on my sixties lingo. My dad told me that back then a lot of people said the word like in front of everything. Like wow! as Lisa wrote in the invitation. Here goes: Like I am definitely coming to the dance. Like Brier Hall is having one, too, but like I don't like Brier Hall girls. Like the sixties is my era, so take me back in a time machine when the "chicks" and guys talked about peace and love and all that! Like that old record by Cher and Sonny—I got you, babe!

Your class trip sounds cool. I think our class trip is scheduled for Williamsburg, Virginia. I'm going to try and get out of it and have my dad send the money he would have paid for that directly to me. I would like to buy an exotic bird with it. Don't ask me why, but I've been into ornithology lately. I saw the most incredible cardinal outside the gym yesterday morning.

Oh yes, about your ghost story—I have a true one. Once when I was staying at my grandparents' house I heard a noise at night in this empty bedroom. Even though I was scared, I went in to check it out. Nobody was there, but it seemed to be coming from the closet. It was one of the old-fashioned kind, like a wardrobe. I think my grandmother called it a chifforobe. Anyway, something definitely wild happened when I opened it up. This small thing dropped on top of my head. I almost had a heart attack, because I had heard that my grandmother's back room was haunted. But somehow I got up the nerve to feel on top of my head to see what this thing was—and it was a lemon peel! Just like that. A lemon peel dropped on top of my head. Now where do you think that could have come from? Only a mystical explanation would suffice. Some spirit was trying to tell me something. Some spirit who liked to eat lemons.

"Like," so long "chick!"
Mars, alias Arthur Martinez

Dear Mars,

You write very good letters. That sixties lingo was a riot! I'm so glad you're coming. Good luck in buying an exotic bird. And thanks for sharing your true ghost story. Maybe it will inspire me.

Yours truly,
Shanon

Dear Sam,

Here is an invitation made by Lisa for The Sixties. I asked the Alma Social Committee to hire you and The Fantasy for the entertainment, but we are having (ugh) piped-in music. The dance should still be lots of fun, and you won't have to do much to yourself since you have long hair already and that's the way some boys used to wear their hair in the sixties. Though I like your hair, I have never much liked the sixties. Perhaps it is because my mother told me once that it was a terrible period and that if my dad had not been a hippie when he was young, the two of them would never have gotten a divorce. I wonder if that's really true. Hope you don't mind my saying something personal about myself.

Guess what? We are going to London! And after that to the dance! What a busy schedule! I'm already trying to plan what to wear and was thinking about shoes. Does Suzy's Shoe Emporium sell old-fashioned shoes? Do you know what kind of shoes they wore back then? Even though I wish they were doing a seventies party, I still have to get a costume for this. I was thinking of buying something in England, but I'd rather buy at your store. Please R.S.V.P. the invitation to the dance as soon as possible.

Fondly,
Palmer Durand

Dear Palmer,

The invitation looks nice. Sorry I can't give you a definite answer until the 17th. The band and I auditioned to be the entertainment for another dance being held on the same night, and I won't know until then whether or not we got the gig. I could kick myself for maybe having to miss a chance at seeing you. Have a great flight to London!

Sincerely,
Sam

P.S. Too bad you can't groove on the sixties. They are my fav. I asked Suzy your question about the shoewear then. She thought it was an odd question. She said something about "go-go boots"—whatever those are—but she doesn't have any in stock. I wish I knew what they looked like so I could help you. Maybe you can find some in England.

Dear Sam,

I am so disappointed that you might not be able to make it to the dance. What is the engagement you and The Fantasy might get on the same night? I hope it's not at Brier Hall. Thank you for the information about the sixties shoes. I will look for them in London. Amy says they have lots of antiques there.

Yours truly,
Palmer

Dear John,

I've been thinking a lot about our argument, and I realize I was wrong. If somebody fooled around with something I wrote, I'd be mad too. I just thought you might like to hear my side of things, since it is a collaboration. But I do not want to risk losing your collaboration and friendship forever. They mean too much to me. Not only that, we made a deal that we would use your words to the song we were writing. Enclosed is a tape in which, if you will pop it into your cassette, you'll hear me singing "Young Willie." This is for your ears only, as I am sensitive about my singing and don't want everyone listening to it. When I sang the song a few times before I made the tape, I realized how definitely nice your words are. I hope you like the music. And I promise I won't change your stuff around again.

We are going to London, which is macro-aggro as far as I see it. Lots of sounds in that place. Enclosed with the tape is an invitation to a dance we are having when we get back. I realize you may not have a sixties costume, since you *usually wear a tie and blazer, but if you do, you can dress for it. I'm not sure what I'm going to do. I don't know if I can get into this costume thing. Anyway, I hope you will come and that you accept this apology, which is a serious one.*

                        Your collaborator again, I hope,
                        Amy Ho

CHAPTER SIX

———◆———

"Tea in Miss Grayson's apartment!" Shanon announced, running into the common room.

Lisa snapped her Latin book shut. "Great! Are there brownies?"

"I don't know," Shanon replied. She tapped Amy's shoulder. "Take off your headphones!" she said loudly.

"What's up?" Amy asked, removing her Walkman.

"Miss Grayson's going to tell us all about the London trip," Shanon said breathlessly. Her eyes gleamed with excitement.

Lisa tugged Shanon's braid. "Is my roomie looking forward to getting on that plane or what?"

"I guess I really am," Shanon said, blushing. "This is definitely the most exciting thing that's ever happened to me. I hope I'm not acting too stupid about it."

"It's good to be excited about things," Amy said, smiling. "I'll go upstairs and tell Palmer to get out of her hot curlers."

"Yes, tell her to hurry," Shanon prompted. "Miss Grayson said as soon as possible!"

The four suitemates, along with Muffin Talbot and the other Fox Hall third-formers, squeezed into Miss Grayson's cozy apartment. A breeze blew in through the window, fluttering crisp white curtains and the bright green leaves of a potted pink geranium on the sill. Miss Grayson, dressed in black slacks and a shirt that was nearly the same violet-blue as her eyes, passed around herb tea and sugar cookies. Leaning into a plushy armchair, Lisa sighed with contentment. "Isn't Miss Grayson's apartment great?" she whispered to Shanon.

"It's wonderful," Shanon whispered back.

"Good cookies," Amy said, gazing up from the floor, where she was sitting cross-legged in front of the couch. Palmer and Muffin Talbot were sharing an ottoman and there were three other girls sprawled on the blue couch.

Just as Miss Grayson was about to begin, the door opened and Kate Majors walked in.

Lisa's face dropped. "What's *she* doing here?" she hissed.

"I think she may be going too," Shanon said softly. "There have to be some upperclassmen to help chaperone us."

"Oh, no," Lisa groaned.

Miss Grayson smiled at the group. "Thank you for coming, girls. The purpose of this little get-together is to give you the latest news on the class trip. By now, your parents have been informed of the plans and fees surrounding the event. I'm glad to say that most of them have responded quickly—and enthusiastically."

43

"Do you know what kind of things we'll be doing in London?" Palmer asked, fluffing out her freshly washed hair.

"The faculty is working on it," said Miss Grayson.

"Will we be going to movies?" Lisa asked, munching a cookie.

Amy raised her hand. "How about concerts?"

Miss Grayson smiled again. "There will be plenty of entertainment on the schedule. We want the trip to be fun for you as well as educational. Mr. Griffith has already ordered our seats for a Shakespearean play!"

"Which one?" asked Amy suspiciously.

Miss Grayson's eyes twinkled. "*Hamlet*."

"Rats," muttered Amy.

"My favorite play," Kate chimed in loudly.

"We'll also be going to Shakespeare's home, Stratford-upon-Avon!" Miss Grayson went on.

"Neat!" Muffin Talbot exclaimed.

"Now, I'm going to pass out a list of recommended wardrobe for the trip," Miss Grayson announced. "One carry-on suitcase, please. And don't forget the raincoats. At this time of the year, England can be quite rainy. . . ."

As Miss Grayson passed out the lists, the girls began to chat among themselves. "I'm beginning to wonder about this trip," Lisa said confidentially. "I didn't realize it was going to be educational! I hope we're not going to have classes on the airplane or anything like that."

"We'd better not," huffed Palmer. "And I notice Miss Grayson didn't say a word about shopping. That's one of the most important things one can do anywhere."

"So is listening to music," Amy added, "and a lot more enjoyable than *Hamlet*."

"We can listen to music and go shopping any time," Shanon argued. "But it's not every day we can go to Shakespeare's birthplace."

When the cookie plate was empty, Miss Grayson got to her feet and said good-bye to everyone. "I'll keep you posted," she called cheerfully. As the girls filed out the door, she touched Shanon's shoulder gently. "Got a minute?"

"Sure," said Shanon.

"I was wondering if you'd spoken to your parents about this," Miss Grayson said as soon as they were alone in the room.

"About the London trip? I wrote to them. I'm sure they'll give their permission."

"Wonderful," said Miss Grayson. "I just hadn't heard back yet on the passport application. Miss Pryn's office is handling all the other details, except for the schedule. That's Mr. Griffith's department. There's so much to think of—tickets, ground transportation, lodging. . . ."

"I think it's really nice of the school to do this for us," Shanon said gratefully. "Not only is it a lot of work, it must cost a lot also."

"The Board of Directors is underwriting a good deal of it," explained Miss Grayson. "The expense left for the parents is quite reasonable."

Shanon swallowed. "The parents have to pay something?"

"Why, yes," said Miss Grayson.

Shanon cleared her throat. "How much?"

"Only a few hundred dollars," Miss Grayson replied.

"A few hundred dollars?" Shanon blinked. "But my par— I mean, I . . . I have to go now. . . ." She darted out of the room.

"Mail call," Amy said, bursting through the door to Suite 3-D. She was wearing her black spandex running suit and carrying a fistful of letters. "I was jogging past Booth Hall, so I figured I'd check out the boxes." She handed a square white envelope to Shanon. "This looks like something from your parents."

Shanon stuck the letter inside her notebook. "Thanks," she said in a worried voice. "I'll look at it later."

"Anything for me?" Lisa asked eagerly. She was arranging Rob's latest picture on top of the sitting-room bookshelf, the place where the Foxes kept most of the memorabilia from their pen pals. Copies of the original ad they'd placed in *The Ardsley Lion*, the first pictures the boys had sent them, a picture of themselves they'd had taken together, even the personality questionnaires they'd sent The Unknown—it was all there.

Amy sat down on the windowsill. "Sorry, nothing for you, Lisa."

Palmer bit her lip. "How about me?"

"Nada," said Amy.

Palmer wrinkled her nose. "Nada? That's the Spanish word for *nothing*, isn't it?" she said fretfully. "Why hasn't Sam written me about Brier Hall? If The Fantasy plays there, I'll just die! After all the trouble I went to in order to have him as a pen pal!"

"Calm down," said Lisa. "Even if he can't make it to The Sixties, I'm sure that Sam will still write to you."

Amy pulled another envelope out of her waist pouch. "Who's that from?" Palmer asked jealously.

"John," Amy replied. She narrowed her eyes. "I wish I had X-ray vision."

"Open it up!" said Lisa. "Don't you want to know what he's written?"

"Not if it's anything like his last letter," Amy retorted.

"That was different," Palmer said.

"This time you sent him the tape," Lisa reminded her.

Amy took a deep breath and ripped open the envelope.

Dear Amy,

When I got that tape you made, I was totally blown away. Your voice is fantastic. You make "Young Willie" sound better than I ever dreamed it could. You make it sound like a real song! And the music is amazing. I played it for Mars and Rob as well as some other guys in Kirby and everybody thought you were a professional. In fact, this guy down the hall named Maxwell Hobart has given me the name of a friend of his—Michael Oliver—who lives somewhere near London. It seems that Michael Oliver is only a few years older than we are, but he's already in the music business. Maxwell says Oliver is always looking for new material, and he thinks our song might be just up his alley. I thought I'd check this out with you. Wouldn't it be great if we could get our song played somewhere or even published? Here is Michael Oliver's address. I am sending the tape back to you. If you agree that we should let this guy hear the song, please mail it. I thought I'd let you make the final decision, since you are so sensitive about your singing. But believe me, you have no reason to be modest. You sound sensational. Anyway, we are selling the song— not your voice—so you shouldn't worry about it. Please let me know right away.

Your collaborator,
John Adams

P.S. I will definitely be at The Sixties. I'm going to write my father and ask him to send me his old wardrobe. He was the original hippie. He was even at Woodstock.

"Fantastic!" Amy cried, jumping up and down. "What a letter!"

"It's the best letter in the world!" exclaimed Lisa. "He even liked your voice!"

Palmer rolled her eyes. "Incredible. I told you that you didn't sound bad."

"It's wonderful," Shanon said quietly.

"All thanks to you," Amy said to Shanon. "You're the one who suggested I make that tape."

Shanon smiled. "I'm glad it worked out," she said, gathering up her books. "Excuse me, I'm going to my room now."

"Don't tell me you're studying again?" Lisa moaned. "With the grades you've been getting, you're going to make the rest of us look like idiots."

"It's not that," Shanon said, smiling weakly. "I have to work some more on my ghost story."

Amy made a comical, scary face. "Ooooo! A ghost story! Maybe we can help you out!"

48

"No thank you," Shanon snapped, shutting the door. "I'd just like to be . . . alone!"

"What's wrong with her?" Palmer said.

"I don't know," said Lisa. "She's been acting mopey ever since we had tea with Miss Grayson."

Amy picked up her guitar. "Maybe it's the ghost story contest. Creativity can be very serious."

Lisa giggled. "Not for you, though. All your songs are so funny."

" 'Cabin Fever' wasn't," Palmer disagreed.

"But that 'Willameena' . . . " Lisa chuckled. "How did you ever think of something so silly?"

For a moment Amy felt hurt, but she covered with a grin. "Yes! Imagine an old lady singing rock and handing out poetry—I guess it is pretty silly. Anyway, no one will ever hear from her again." She smiled and tucked John's letter away. "Willameena the Bard is dead."

Long after the lights were out in Lisa and Shanon's room, Lisa heard her roommate tossing in bed.

"Shanon?" she whispered. "Are you awake?"

"I can't sleep," Shanon said softly.

Lisa turned over. "What's wrong? Is something bothering you?"

"It's that letter from home," Shanon said.

Lisa flicked on her flashlight. "What did it say? Is your mom or dad sick?"

"Nothing like that," Shanon replied, staring up at the ceiling. "Actually, I haven't opened the letter yet. Because I know what it's going to say and I just can't—"

"Hey!" Lisa said, jumping out of bed. "You're not crying, are you?"

Shanon wiped her eyes with the tail of the sheet. "I feel so silly. But I really did want to go. I knew it was too good to be true."

"What are you talking about?" asked Lisa.

Shanon tried to compose herself. "The trip to England is going to cost several hundred dollars. Miss Grayson told me. I thought the school would be paying for it."

Lisa shrugged. "The school *is* paying for most of it."

"But not enough," Shanon said helplessly. "I can't expect my parents to shell out that kind of money for a trip. There are four other children in my family. And Doreen's in college this semester."

"Oh, wow," Lisa murmured sympathetically. "I see what you mean."

Shanon reached for the letter from her parents. It was still in her notebook on the night table. "I might as well read this, I guess."

Dear Shanon,

Your father and I are thrilled about your opportunity to go to London. Miss Pryn and the school were so helpful. Though Dad and I were bound and determined you would go, at first it seemed tight. But then we contacted the school and Miss Pryn's office was very nice and made the fee more affordable for our budget. You must really be doing good work over there at Alma Stephens! We are all proud of you. Have fun.

With love,
Mom

Shanon plopped her head back onto the pillow and let out a big sigh of relief. Then she grinned at Lisa. "I can't believe it—I'm really going to London!"

CHAPTER SEVEN

Dear John,

Thanks for your great letter. Also thanks for the compliments about my voice. I have always put myself down about my voice—especially since I got kicked out of Chorus for not reading music. But I hear a lot of people with musical genius can't read music. Of course, I'm not saying I'm one of those, but you never know. Anyway, I am sending the tape of our song to Michael Oliver. I can hardly wait for him to answer. Isn't it an incredible coincidence that he lives in London and that's where we are going? Maybe I'll even get to meet him! Thank you again. Feels great to be your collaborator.

Your pen pal,
Amy

Dear Amy,

I'm glad you decided to send the tape to Michael Oliver. Let me know if you hear from him. He does know that both of us wrote the song and not just you, doesn't he? Just checking.

Your pen pal,
John

Dear Michael Oliver,

My name is Amy Ho and I am a friend of a friend of Maxwell Hobart. I have written the music to a song with a collaborator John Adams who goes to Ardsley Academy and knows Maxwell. John and I were hoping that you might listen to this tape of our song since Maxwell says you are always on the lookout for new material. If you could answer soon, I would appreciate it. My class at Alma Stephens School for Girls (which is across the river from Ardsley) is about to go to London for a week.

Yours truly,
Amy Elizabeth Ho

Dear Amy Elizabeth,

How nice to get your letter. And I must say that your tape was sensational. Who is the vocalist? Anyone I've heard of? Her sound is truly unique. Definitely not your whiny soprano type. I love girls' voices when they are deep like that. In any case, please send me her name so I can get some of her recordings. About the song you wrote with this chap John—it's really quite nice. Would you mind if my band and I fiddled around with it? It might be just the thing for one of our Rock Teas. My father has a small lunch place in Stratford-upon-Avon. He is incredibly supportive of me and the group and lets us have music sessions there each Thursday at four. All my friends come in to play their instruments or just to listen. I am sending you a flyer with a picture of our group, Dead Times. I am the bloke in the middle wearing the black beret. The girl in the white dress with the zither is my sister Pamela. Thanks again for sending me your song.

Best wishes and Cheerio,
Michael Oliver

Dear Michael Oliver,

The three girls I live with and I were very excited to hear what you do at your father's restaurant. I see from the flyer it's called The Sandwich Board. Your group looks incredible. Why is it called Dead Times? Does your sister Pamela play rock on the zither? By the way, you cannot buy any recordings of the vocalist on the tape I sent you because it was me who was singing. Thanks a lot for the compliments! I hope you don't mind, but my roommates and I would like to come to The Sandwich Board when we are in London. I am going to tell John how much you liked our song. I'm sure he won't mind if your band wants to play it.

Yours truly,
Amy Elizabeth

Dear Amy Elizabeth,

The telephone number of The Sandwich Board is on the flyer I sent you. Glad you like the way the group looks. We really are rather a motley crew. And yes, Pamela does play rock on the zither. We call ourselves Dead Times because we are located in Stratford-upon-Avon, a wonderful place.

Though Shakespeare is dead, here his times live forever. So, you see, the name is not a bit morbid to us. In Shakespeare's day, the musicians and writers were true artistic souls. From the sound of your voice, so are you. How long have you been performing? I'd love to meet you and your roomies. Call me when you get to London, and we'll arrange something.

Michael Oliver

Dear John,

You will not believe what has happened!!!! I wrote to Michael Oliver like you said I should and sent him the tape and he loved it! He loved my voice! He said I was a true artistic soul and—get this—he doesn't understand why I'm not making records. He and his sister Pamela get together with their friends to jam every week in their father's restaurant. Palmer, Lisa, Shanon, and I will definitely try to check it out. Who knows? Maybe they'll be playing our song. Michael Oliver certainly is interested. He has already written me two humongous letters. I wrote back, of course. I can hardly wait to meet him. See you at The Sixties when we get back!

Amy Elizabeth

Dear Amy,

Who is Amy Elizabeth? Is that your middle name or something? I hope I didn't make a mistake by having you write to this Michael Oliver. I don't understand why he's so interested in our song. I certainly hope he's not going to do anything to change it. Remember how hard it was for

us to come to an agreement on the final version. I'm glad
he thinks your voice is great. I have asked my father to
send a costume for The Sixties.

John

Dear John,
    I'm sure we can trust Michael Oliver. He was writing a
lot not only because of our song, but because he thought
my voice was so great. I signed myself Amy Elizabeth,
because that is what he called me in his letters. Isn't that
English? Almost like Queen Elizabeth, ha-ha. If there's
enough time before the London trip, I will write to
Michael Oliver again to make sure he doesn't change our
song in his arrangement.

Yours truly,
Amy

Dear Amy,
    You must be spending a lot of postage writing to this guy
Michael Oliver. Anybody would think you had a new pen
pal. Have fun in London.

Your collaborator,
John

P.S. I like plain Amy better than Amy Elizabeth. Amy
Elizabeth doesn't sound at all like you.

CHAPTER EIGHT

———◆———

"The night was dark and spooky," Shanon said. "The air was cold and had a damp quality. The heroine thought it was like the skin of lizards. She stepped up to ring the doorbell. Her hand was shaking. All her life she'd been afraid of Mrs. Hubbard. Even the grown people in the neighborhood thought that there was something strange about the old lady—that she had a special power. Not only that, her wooden white house was haunted. The shutters flapped in the wind as the heroine of our story—"

"That's enough," yawned Lisa. "You're scaring me."

The four Foxes and the rest of the Alma freshman class were on their way to London. High above the Atlantic, the big airplane they had boarded back in the States soared through the night sky. Having finished her airline dinner and watched the movie *Halloween*, Palmer was already napping. But her three suitemates were much too excited to sleep, so Shanon was entertaining Lisa and Amy by reading them her ghost story.

Shanon gave Lisa a suspicious look. "Don't try to make me feel good. I know my story isn't scary yet. I had no idea how hard it would be to make up something spooky. Just think how hard it must have been to write *Halloween*."

"Yes, it *was* pretty scary for an airplane movie," Lisa agreed.

"What's scary to me is being so high up in the sky," Shanon confided. "I like the feeling of the ground underneath my feet."

"Relax," said Amy. "Don't think about it."

Suddenly the airplane lurched slightly. The voice of the stewardess came over the speaker: "Sorry, ladies and gentlemen. We're experiencing some slight turbulence. The captain requests that you fasten your seat belts."

"Turbulence?" said Shanon in a shaky voice. "What's that?"

"Air currents," Amy replied nonchalantly. "Go on with your story."

"Not now," Shanon said, tucking the notebook into her bag. "It's scary enough with all this turbulence."

"I'm going to get some shut-eye," Lisa said, putting one of the airline pillows behind her head.

"I thought you were going to stay awake through the whole trip," Amy teased.

"Miss Grayson asked us to get some rest," Lisa said defensively. "Otherwise we'll be too tired tomorrow."

"You sleep," said Amy, "not me. I'm wired."

"Me too," said Shanon. "My heart's beating."

Lisa giggled. "It's always beating, silly. That's why

you're alive." She bunched up the pillow and tried to get comfortable. "Good night."

Amy and Shanon were quiet for a moment. Most of the overhead lamps in the plane had been turned off. On the other side of Lisa, Palmer burrowed under a blanket.

"Is Palmer's seat belt fastened?" Shanon asked in concern.

"She never unsnapped it," Amy answered. Across the aisle Kate was sitting with Muffin Talbot.

According to Shanon's watch, it wasn't even dinnertime, but outside the window it was already dark. "I wish we could see down below," she said.

"All we'd see is water," said Amy. "The Atlantic Ocean."

"Sounds cold." Shanon shivered.

"Don't be scared," Amy said. "Before you know it, we'll be in England."

The seat belt light went off and Miss Grayson left her place next to Mr. Griffith. "Everything okay here?" she whispered to Amy and Shanon.

"We're fine," Amy answered. "Only I'm thirsty."

Miss Grayson smiled. "I'll see if the stewardess can bring you more sodas. I'm sure she won't mind. Most of the other passengers are sound asleep."

"Is Mr. Griffith asleep?" Amy asked curiously.

"Yes, he's even snoring," Miss Grayson said with a chuckle.

Amy and Shanon giggled.

"Want to play a game?" Amy asked when Miss Grayson had left to find the stewardess.

"I suppose it'll kill time," said Shanon.

"Truth or dare?" said Amy.

Shanon giggled. "Truth!"

"Okay," challenged Amy. "What are you thinking this very moment?"

Shanon felt her face redden. "How much I miss Mars."

"You're kidding," laughed Amy. "We're not even off the airplane. And even when you're at Alma, you hardly ever see him."

"That doesn't matter. We're still a lot farther away now. I wonder if he's bought his exotic bird yet."

Amy laughed again. "I bet he has."

"Yes," Shanon sighed. "He's very resourceful. Okay, your turn—truth or dare?"

Amy shrugged. "Truth."

Shanon turned in her seat. "I'll ask you the same question," she said mischievously. "What's on your mind this very minute?"

"The Sandwich Board," Amy announced without hesitation.

Shanon's eyes twinkled. "The Sandwich Board or that guy who has the teas there, Michael Oliver?"

"Just The Sandwich Board," said Amy. "But I must admit, Michael Oliver looked quite interesting in that picture he sent."

"More interesting than John?" Shanon prodded.

Amy thought for a moment. "No. I don't know Michael Oliver. John's already a friend, even though it is hard to figure him out sometimes."

The plane jolted again. This time, Shanon hardly flinched. "More turbulence, right?"

Amy smiled at her. "You're getting the hang of it."

"Thanks for calming me down before," Shanon said gratefully.

"That's okay," said Amy. "I get scared about some things too."

"Like what?" asked Shanon. "What's the scariest thing you could ever think of doing?"

Amy thought. "Singing in front of a bunch of people."

"But you sing in front of us all the time," Shanon said in surprise.

"That's because you're my friends," Amy admitted. "Anyway, my voice is weird-sounding."

"Come on," said Shanon. "You're being too modest. John and his friends and Michael Oliver all think you have an absolutely incredible voice."

Amy flushed. "That's true."

"So why should you be scared to sing in front of anyone?" Shanon continued.

Amy felt suddenly light-headed. "Maybe you're right. If I sound as great as everybody says I do, there's really nothing to be afraid of."

"Who knows?" said Shanon. "Perhaps someday you'll be discovered."

"Why not?" Amy said, pleased at the prospect. "Maybe I will be discovered. Maybe I'm a born performer."

Shanon reached for a pillow. "I have a feeling you are," she said. "I never told you, but I liked your song about the old lady Willameena."

"Really?" said Amy. "It seemed sort of special when I first thought of it."

"You've got a good imagination," Shanon said, yawning.

"I wish I had one. I still can't figure out how to describe the scary lady in my ghost story. I can't just say she's scary. I have to write down what she looks like. How do you make your brain do that kind of thing?"

"Who knows?" Amy murmured, struggling to keep her eyes open. "It's something that sort of happens . . . by itself . . . at least I think so. . . ."

Lisa and Palmer were already sleeping soundly. And soon Amy and Shanon dropped off to sleep, too. Even Miss Grayson's eyes shut for a moment. The hum of the plane lulled them all. Lisa dreamed that she was at a big dance with Rob. Shanon dreamed of a pet store with exotic birds, while Palmer dreamed about shoes. In Amy's dream, she stood on a stage singing, while people all around applauded her. She wasn't a bit afraid. In fact, she was fearless. Then someone in the audience stood up and gave her a card. It was an old woman dressed in blue with mischievous eyes. Bold blue letters on the card spelled out *Willameena*. . . .

"Good morning, ladies and gentlemen. Welcome to Heathrow Airport. On behalf of the captain and the rest of the crew I'd like to thank you for flying with us. We hope your stay in England will be a memorable one. Before deplaning, you can set your watches to local time. It is now six o'clock A.M."

"Six o'clock in the morning!" Shanon exclaimed. "We stayed up almost all night!"

"It's the time change," said Lisa, rubbing her eyes. "Actually, back in the United States it's pretty late, too. One o'clock."

"One o'clock in the morning?" Palmer said, stretching. "Boy, is my body stiff!"

Miss Grayson, Mr. Griffith, and the other faculty hurried along the aisles. "Don't forget anything," Miss Grayson called cheerfully.

"Check those front seat pockets," Mr. Griffith advised. "And the overhead compartments. Everyone put your coats on, then remain seated."

Amy reached under the seat for her knapsack. "Wow, did I ever have a dream," she said, blinking.

"What was it?" Shanon asked.

"I can't exactly remember," Amy replied, "but it was a doozy."

On signal, several rows of Alma girls rose from their seats. With Mr. Griffith in the lead, Miss Grayson in the middle, and Miss Dewar and Mr. Seganish bringing up the rear, they filed off the plane. As they left, the stewardess and captain shook each of their hands. Then they had to stand in line at customs for what seemed like hours. But finally they stepped out into the early dawn and onto English soil.

It was drizzling but surprisingly mild. A light mist cooled the girls' faces as a bus pulled up to take them to their hotel.

"Everyone stay together," Miss Grayson cautioned. "Please form a line to get on the bus."

Shanon squeezed Lisa's arm. "Wow," she murmured, "this is so exciting."

"Yes, it is," said Lisa, feeling the thrill. "We're really in England!"

CHAPTER NINE

———◆———

Dear Rob,
   I am writing this letter to you half asleep. Of course it is evening, but I feel like it's late at night. I have been feeling that way ever since we arrived in London. Miss Grayson says I have jet lag! Amy didn't seem to get it and neither did Shanon, and Palmer takes so many naps back at Alma, I guess she was too well rested. But I've got it bad. I am looking at my watch and it says seven o'clock in the evening, but back in New Hampshire where you are, it's only two in the afternoon. Usually at this time, I have just finished lunch, but here in England I have just finished dinner. Of course, the menu isn't that different. We had bangers and mash this evening, ha-ha! That's just what Mrs. Butter serves us at lunchtime. Even so, my stomach still feels like it ought to be eating lunch and not dinner. I also feel there ought to be a lot more hours in the day, but soon it's going to be dark. It will be bedtime and I won't

be at all sleepy. Last night everybody got to sleep but me. I was still wide awake at 4:30 A.M. I guess that's because back home in New Hampshire, it was only 11:30 P.M.! I hope I will soon adjust to these changes.

Our hotel is very nice. It's located in a section of London called Bloomsbury. A lot of artists used to live here, including Charles Dickens! In fact, we've already gone to visit his old house. It's just a few blocks away from our hotel. You can't imagine how strange it felt to be in the same place where the great author once lived! As we walked up an old wooden staircase to the top floor, I kept thinking, Dickens used to walk up those same stairs! I was very impressed by that. I also was impressed by some old letters that were framed in one room. They were written by Charles Dickens himself in his own handwriting. They were about the time his wife's sister died. She was a very young woman and quite pretty. It was sad.

I really miss you, Rob, but this trip is more special than I ever expected. We haven't seen any movies at all yet. We are too busy going to museums. I never much liked going to museums in the United States, but in England for some reason I do. I am becoming a real anglophile—that means a lover of things that are English. I will see you when I get back.

Cheerio,
Lisa

Dear Mars,
Everywhere I look in England, I see my favorite color—green! It hasn't rained that much since we've been here,

but the lady at the desk in our hotel said it poured a bundle before then. So that is why there is so much green grass everywhere. Not only that, London isn't cold at all. The winter was especially mild this year. And there are already flowers! I love flowers.

Our hotel is great! Lisa, Palmer, Amy, and I are sharing adjoining doubles—just like at Alma. It's great. We're so used to living together. There are so many of us on tour that we practically fill the whole place. (The hotel is not one of those huge ones. It's medium size.) Every morning, we get up and have a huge English breakfast—cereal and eggs and bacon and sausage and toast and jam. We also have pots of tea on the tables with real cream! Oh, I forgot—we have juice also.

Everyone's having a wonderful time. Even Miss Grayson and Mr. Griffith seem to be getting a vacation out of this, though they do have a lot of responsibility. Imagine, keeping track of so many people! Of course, we aren't exactly kindergartners, and Mr. Seganish and Miss Dewar are here too. But, still, I wouldn't like to be in charge of so many girls.

It's hard to pick out the favorite sights we've seen. There have been so many already: Big Ben (you wouldn't believe how big that clock is), Piccadilly Circus, and St. Paul's Cathedral, to name just a few. The whole trip seems planned down to the minute.

I still can't believe I'm actually here! It is like a dream. Even my parents have never been to Europe. I want them to go, because I think they would like it. By the way, I wish you were here, too. After this, I know I will visit other places in Europe—especially now that I have my very own passport! Do you have your own passport? Maybe you'll go traveling, too!—at the same time I do.

Smitten with London,
Shanon

Dear Sam,

It is quite romantic here, especially the stores. There are so many beautiful sweaters and flowered print dresses. I am still trying to find the right shoes for the sixties dance. We also went to a gigantic toy store named Hamley's. I got a little doll for Gabby—the girl I've been tutoring for my community-service project at Alma. After hanging around London for a couple of days, we went on a day trip to Windsor Castle. The royal state apartments are open to the public. I never saw such fabulous furniture in my whole life! And the walls were practically covered with paintings. My mother would have liked it, since she collects art. But even she doesn't have a collection like this. While I was walking through the rooms, I kept pretending that I lived there. I know that nobody except kings and queens lives in castles anymore, but I couldn't help wishing. We weren't allowed to sit in the chairs because they were so old and valuable, but I kept trying to imagine that they belonged to me and that if I really wanted to, I could sit down in them. Also at Windsor, there was an amazing doll house! It was so huge you had to walk around it to see the whole thing. And it had so many rooms I could hardly count them. But the most amazing thing of all was that every single room was filled with tiny doll furniture. And I mean tiny! There was a sewing basket with some scissors in it as small as a baby's fingernail. A real little girl used to play with those things, I guess. Anyway, it all belonged to her—to Queen Mary. I am enjoying myself, but looking forward very much to seeing you again. Though lately my roommate's singing has been droning in my ear, I still think of your voice and the sound of The Fantasy.

Yours, though far away,
Palmer

Dear John,

I haven't seen Michael Oliver yet, but London is a truly rad place! I have already had two unbelievable experiences. One in the Guinness World of Records, where I saw pictures of the fattest and tallest people in the world as well as phenomenal athletes. The other one was in this place called the National Portrait Gallery. There are hundreds and hundreds of pictures of famous people there! After a while, you feel that they are not just portraits but actual people. There are so many faces. I liked the portraits of Charles Dickens and the Brontë sisters a lot. But most of all, I liked the one of Shakespeare. I think it's one of the only portraits of him that was actually done from real life. And you know what? He looked like an ordinary person. He was such a famous writer and even now, long after he's dead, people enjoy his plays. But he didn't look stuck up or affected. He just looked like a real human being. With very deep eyes.

Back to the twentieth century, the dress code has been relaxed while we are here. We can wear pants, so long as our jackets are coordinated. So I'm wearing all black leather! Ha-ha! Wish me luck in getting to The Sandwich Board. Talk about coordination, every second of this trip is planned. Every day we go somewhere else—usually by bus even if it's not that far away. What can I say? It's a school trip, but still quite incredible. I think we are all kind of dumbstruck. And getting sort of English. We are eating fish and chips as well as bangers and calling the bathroom the loo, just like the Brits do. I just hope I can arrange to meet Michael Oliver. Getting to a pay phone is almost impossible. And the two times I called Stratford-upon-Avon, either Michael Oliver wasn't at The Sandwich Board or the line was busy. But don't worry, I'll keep trying.

Yours truly,
Amy

CHAPTER TEN

Lined up in twos, the group from Alma filed out of their elegant, old hotel. The street was wide and full of traffic, and across the way was a large, green park full of blossoms. Kate Majors stood on the sidewalk right outside the hotel. Miss Grayson was at the door of the red double-decker tour bus that took them on their daily sightseeing trips.

"Can I mail these?" Lisa asked Kate, breaking out of line and waving a fistful of postcards.

"You know the rules," Kate said. "You're not supposed to leave the group."

"I should have known you would say that," Lisa protested. "Come on," she pleaded, "the post office is right on the corner. I don't even have to cross the street!"

Kate got flustered and waved the line on. "I don't know," she said. The post office was only a few yards away, but she wasn't sure what Miss Grayson might say about it. "We'll find another place to mail your postcards," Kate hedged. "Maybe at the museum."

Lisa stood her ground. "I think you're being unreasonable," she persisted as Shanon, Amy, and Palmer left the line boarding the bus and joined her.

"Now, why are you all lagging?" Kate asked shrilly.

"We have some postcards to mail," explained Amy.

"I would take them to the post office for you," Lisa pouted, "but Kate won't let me go—even though it's just at the corner."

"Why not, Kate?" asked Palmer. "She wouldn't even have to go inside. There's a mail slot right on the outside of the building. Anyway, I have some things to mail too."

"So do I," Shanon added politely.

"Who knows when we'll pass another mailbox," said Amy.

Kate looked toward the bus and sighed. The rest of the class had all boarded. "I don't make the rules," she explained.

"What's going on there?" Miss Grayson called from the curb.

And Mr. Griffith stuck his head out of the bus door. "Don't dally, please."

"We're coming," Kate replied, hurrying the four Foxes along.

Suddenly, Lisa dashed up ahead. "May I run to the post office and mail some cards?" she asked Miss Grayson directly. "Please, it's only at the corner."

Miss Grayson smiled and reached into her purse. "Sure, but don't be long. And, while you're at it, drop this off

71

too." She handed Lisa a postcard with a picture of Westminster Abbey on the front. Collecting Amy's, Shanon's, and Palmer's mail as well, Lisa shot down to the corner, threw the cards into the slot, and ran back again.

"Thanks, Miss Grayson," she said, boarding the bus. Quickly climbing to the top level, she settled into the seat Shanon had saved for her. Across the aisle sat Amy and Palmer. Kate was right in front of them.

"Thanks for mailing my postcard," Amy hissed across the aisle.

"Thank Miss Grayson for allowing me to," Lisa said pointedly. "I should have asked her in the first place. She's not a maniac for rules like some people. And she's a teacher."

Kate's ears got red. She knew Lisa had said that for her benefit and it really upset her. It was awful to realize that Reggie's sister actually thought of her as a rule maniac.

As the double-decker bus made its way down a busy street, Shanon and Palmer looked out the window.

"I still can't get used to seeing the traffic on the left side of the street," Shanon remarked nervously. "I keep thinking a car is going to crash into us."

"Who cares about the traffic!" said Palmer. "I can't believe we're passing all these great stores without stopping to shop."

"Which museum are we going to this morning?" Lisa asked, rummaging through her bag for her schedule.

"The British Museum," Shanon replied. She'd already memorized the whole thing. "Miss Grayson says they have a gigantic Egyptian collection. I can't wait to see the mummies!"

"What I can't wait for," Amy chimed in, "is Stratford-upon-Avon!"

Mr. Griffith turned around in his seat ahead of them. "Glad to hear you're so eager to visit Shakespeare's old stomping grounds!" he called over the rumble of the bus motor. "It's planned for tomorrow."

"I know," Amy called out eagerly. "I'm really excited."

"Wonderful," said Mr. Griffith. "You'll love the birthplace."

Amy drew a blank. "The what?"

"The birthplace!" replied Mr. Griffith. "The house where William Shakespeare was born."

"Oh, right!" said Amy, settling back in her seat.

"Have you asked whether we can visit The Sandwich Board yet?" Lisa whispered.

"Not yet," Amy said quietly. "I want to get through to Michael Oliver first," she explained as the bus pulled up outside a huge, formidable old building.

"What's this?" Palmer asked, blinking. "It looks like Buckingham Palace."

"Not quite," Lisa giggled. "It's the museum."

"Oh," said Palmer. She got up from her seat and collected her navy blue blazer. "We've been seeing so many big old buildings, I'm getting cross-eyed. They all look the same to me."

The group climbed off the bus and lined up again. While Mr. Griffith went ahead to alert the tour guide of their arrival, Miss Grayson walked down the row of girls, counting heads again.

"How long are we going to be here?" Palmer asked the young teacher. "I want to get in some more shopping."

"We won't be shopping again until the very last day," Miss Grayson replied. She checked out the name tag on Palmer's blazer. "I'm glad to see that you're all wearing your identification tags."

As Miss Grayson moved on, Lisa tried unsuccessfully to smother a giggle.

"What's so funny?" asked Amy.

Lisa chuckled. "I just think it's weird the way they have us wearing these ID badges," she answered.

"I know what you mean," Palmer said, rolling her eyes. "You'd think we were five years old."

"They must think the badges make us more official-looking," Shanon volunteered. "Or maybe they're afraid we'll get lost."

Palmer raised an eyebrow. "Lost? If that happened, I could tell somebody my own name. I don't need it written down on a badge."

"Anyway," said Amy, "I don't see how any of us could ever get lost here. Every five minutes we're standing in line somewhere getting our heads counted."

The tour guide for the Alma group finally appeared and the long line of girls and their teachers entered the museum. While the other girls exclaimed over the impressive-looking building, Amy kept her eyes peeled for a telephone. She saw one almost immediately. Skipping ahead in line, she grabbed Kate by the elbow.

"Hey Kate," she exclaimed. "There's a telephone back there. Can I use it?"

"You know I can't give you permission," Kate answered, not slowing her pace. "If you leave the group, you might get lost."

74

"I'm not going to get lost!" Amy protested as the group kept moving. "There's a bathroom!" she said, grasping at straws. "You can't refuse me permission to use that."

Kate finally slowed down. "I suppose not," she said grudgingly. "I'll go up ahead and tell Miss Grayson and then come back for you."

Amy smiled. "Thanks a lot." She ducked into the ladies' room, then ducked back out. The Alma group was no longer in sight. Running through the museum corridor, Amy made a beeline for the unoccupied pay telephone, deposited a ten pence piece, and frantically dialed Michael Oliver's telephone number. She tapped her foot impatiently while the phone rang. Any minute, she knew, Kate would come looking for her. Someone finally answered the phone at the other end.

"Hello?" a girl's voice said.

"Hello! This is Amy Ho. May I speak to Michael Oliver?"

There was a moment's silence.

"Amy Elizabeth?" the girl's voice piped up pleasantly. "The songwriter?"

Amy flushed with pleasure. "Yes, that's me. Who is this?"

"Pamela Oliver, Michael's sister," the girl replied. "Michael played us your tape. Dead Times thinks you're wonderful!"

"Thanks," said Amy, flattered. She glanced down the corridor. "Uh . . . I'm sort of in a hurry. Is Michael there? I've been trying to reach him for days."

"He's still in school," Pamela explained. "I would be,

too, but we had half day today. You can reach him after three thirty, however."

Amy swallowed her disappointment. "Okay, I'll try to call back then. Could you tell him that tomor—"

Suddenly there was a loud beeping noise in Amy's ear. A flashing sign appeared on the phone, telling her to insert more money. She stuck her hand into her pocket for another ten pence, and dropped it into the coin slot. The beeping stopped.

"Are you there?" Pamela asked.

"Yes," said Amy breathlessly. "I'm sorry. I didn't put in enough money. Could you please just tell Michael that we're going to be in Stratford-upon-Avon tomorrow, but I—"

Once again Amy was interrupted. But this time it was Kate, tapping her on the shoulder. Amy jerked in surprise. She hadn't seen her coming.

"Ladies' room, huh?" Kate said, tapping her foot.

"I'm sorry," Amy said, muffling the phone. "I'll be finished in a—"

The phone began to beep again. Amy sighed in frustration. "Listen, Pamela," she said in a loud voice, trying to make herself heard above the beeping. "I'll call later."

"Is there somewhere Michael can reach you?" Pamela asked.

For a split second the beeping stopped and it was quiet. "No," said Amy, still shouting. "We don't have a phone in our hotel room and we're never there anyway. I'll have to try again."

"Cheerio, then!" said Pamela.

"Ditto," Amy said in her normal voice. "Cheerio."

Avoiding Kate's accusing glance, Amy hung up the phone. There was a long moment of silence.

"That was a very important telephone call," Amy finally said, lifting her eyes to face Kate.

The older girl adjusted her glasses. "Then why did you lie? Why didn't you just say you had a very important call to make?"

"Because it wouldn't have made a difference," Amy said, seething. "I asked you if I could use the phone, and you said no. That's why I made up the excuse about the ladies' room."

Kate thought for a minute, then shrugged. "Oh, well. No harm done."

Amy sighed in relief. "Thanks. So, you won't tell Miss Grayson?"

Kate shrugged again. "Why should I? Come on, let's go to the gift shop."

Amy followed Kate down the corridor. "Is that where everybody else is?" she asked. "In the gift shop?"

"No, they've gone upstairs to one of the Egyptian rooms," Kate answered. She pulled a map out of her raincoat pocket. "I know what room they're in. We can catch up with them later."

Inside the museum shop, Kate headed straight for the postcards. "There's a friend I wanted to get a nice card for," she told Amy. "I don't know if Miss Grayson and Mr. Griffith are planning to stop here."

Browsing through the postcards, Amy selected one of a vividly painted mummy case. She was glad to have the unscheduled shopping opportunity, but there was something about Kate's attitude that was really getting to her.

"How come you don't have to ask permission to go buy postcards, but I have to ask permission to go to the ladies' room, and I'm not even allowed to make a telephone call?" Amy couldn't help asking.

Kate glanced at her. "Because I'm older than you are," she replied simply. "And on this trip, I have a position of authority."

"Hmph!" Amy snorted, marching over to the cashier.

"Don't feel bad," Kate said, smiling good-naturedly. "Freshmen are always treated like babies. I was. You'll get more freedom next year. Besides, right now you're in a foreign country."

"Anybody would think the English didn't speak the same language we do," Amy complained. "Miss Grayson will hardly let us out of her sight."

"That's natural under the circumstances," Kate said, paying for her postcard. The cashier put the card in a small bag, but Kate took it out again to show Amy. "Nice mummy picture, huh?"

Amy nodded. "Interesting. I got one, too."

"For who?" Kate asked curiously. "Your pen pal?"

"Yes," Amy replied, smiling. She paused for a moment. "Who's yours for?"

Kate turned beet red. "For a friend at Ardsley."

"Lisa's brother Reggie?" Amy asked, enjoying Kate's embarrassment.

Kate's face was still red. "Uh-huh." She motioned toward the door. "We'd better get upstairs now."

The girls walked quickly out of the shop and down the corridor. "This is a really exceptional museum," Kate said. "There's actually a copy of the Magna Carta in one of these rooms!"

"Wow!" said Amy. "That's ancient." She was quiet for a moment as they hurried up the wide staircase. "Hey, Kate," she began hesitantly. "I may have a problem."

"What's that?" the older girl asked.

"The person I was calling . . . is somebody I wanted to see while we're in England," Amy confided. "He lives in Stratford-upon-Avon."

"We're going there tomorrow," said Kate.

"I know," said Amy in a rush. "And I *have* to see him! I really do! It's very important for me and my pen pal."

As the girls entered one of the Egyptian rooms, Amy spotted the Alma group in a far corner.

"I hate to tell you this," Kate said, "but I don't see how you can do that."

Amy bit her lip. "I knew you'd say that. I don't even know why I bothered to tell you about it."

Kate stared at her. "Why do you say that? Because you think I'm a rule maniac?"

Amy felt herself flush. Kate must have overheard Lisa's remark.

"I don't necessarily think that about you," said Amy.

"But Lisa does," Kate confronted her.

"I guess so," Amy muttered.

Just then, Miss Grayson caught Kate's eye and waved from the far corner. Kate nudged Amy, and they started toward the group.

"Listen!" Kate whispered, grabbing Amy's arm suddenly. "I'd help you see your friend if I could. Honest!"

"You would?" Amy said in surprise. "Then why don't you?"

Kate shrugged helplessly. "How?"

"Ask Miss Grayson and Mr. Griffith if we can stop at my friend's father's restaurant in Stratford-upon-Avon tomorrow," Amy pleaded.

"Why don't you ask yourself?" Kate said quickly.

"Because they'd probably listen to you more," Amy replied, stopping in front of a mummy case. "This is very important to me. I don't know when I'll ever get to London again."

Kate gazed at the mummy case. "I'll ask Miss Grayson about it," she said quietly. "On one condition."

"What's that?" Amy asked eagerly.

Kate turned her gaze to the Alma group. Lisa was standing next to Mr. Griffith. "Just tell Lisa that I'm going to bat for you," Kate said. "I want her to—"

"I get it!" Amy broke in, smiling. "You want Lisa to know that even though you're a rule maniac, you're also a nice person?"

Kate smiled. "Something like that," she said as they rejoined the group at last.

After the museum tour, the Alma girls had lunch in a nearby restaurant. Over heaping plates of fish and chips, Amy told Lisa, Shanon, and Palmer about her conversation with Kate.

"That's really nice of Kate to say she'd try to help you,"

80

Lisa said. She munched a chip thoughtfully. "Of course, it remains to be seen whether she can convince Mr. Griffith and Miss Grayson to let you go to The Sandwich Board."

"She has to!" said Amy dramatically.

After lunch the group strolled through a beautiful park with a pond. They bought balloons and hot chocolate, saw a mother swan with brand-new babies, and from a distance, saw a punky-looking girl with orange hair, high black boots, and a leopard-skin coat.

"Wow, is she ever punked out!" laughed Palmer.

"I think she looks great," Amy exclaimed.

"Shhh!" said Shanon. "She's coming our way!"

The punked-out girl ambled by and handed Palmer a sheet of bright pink paper.

"Oh, my gosh!" Palmer said. "It's an advertisement for a shoe store called Willameena's! Now, where have I heard that name before?" she giggled, elbowing Amy.

Smiling at the punky-looking girl, Amy took a flyer too.

"Check us out, love," the girl said warmly. "We're located right in the middle of Piccadilly Circus."

"We're going to be there on our last day," said Palmer, "aren't we, Amy?"

But Amy had already stuck the flyer in her pocket and was walking away. Just outside the park, she'd spied a pay phone. This time when she asked Kate if she could make a call, Kate gave her permission.

"Did you tell Lisa I was going to try to help you?" Kate whispered.

Amy nodded. "Yes. She thought it was really nice of you." Motioning over to where her friends were still clustered around the girl with the leopard-skin coat, she said, "Lisa's right over there. Why don't you go talk to her?"

"I think I will," Kate said, blushing.

As she headed toward the pay phone, Amy couldn't help grinning. She absentmindedly sang a few bars of her song "Willameena," marveling at the coincidence of that being the name of the punky girl's shoe store.

This time when she called the number in Stratford-upon-Avon, a boy's voice answered.

"Michael Oliver here."

Amy caught her breath. "Uh ... Yes ... I ... this is Amy."

"Amy Elizabeth!" he exclaimed. "Glad to hear your voice, girl! Where are you?"

"In London," she answered, swallowing. "But tomorrow we'll be in Stratford."

Michael Oliver chuckled. "Smashing! What time will you be popping over?"

"Uh, I'm not sure," Amy replied. "Can I call you when we get there? We're on a very tight schedule."

"Righto," Michael said. "Just make certain that we won't miss you. It would be a dreadful disappointment to us all—Pam, myself, and Dead Times, too."

"Sounds great," Amy said. "I'll call you tomorrow. I'm pretty sure we can manage to come over."

"Until then," he said warmly. "And don't forget ... bring your friends!"

"Wow!" Amy cried, hanging up the phone. She'd finally managed to speak with him! Not only that, he had sounded genuinely glad to hear from her. And suddenly she was absolutely positive that Kate would get permission for her to meet him.

Amy jogged back through the park in high spirits. She could hardly wait to send John a postcard, telling him the big news. Stopping at the refreshment stand, she bought another hot chocolate. Lisa was talking with Kate now, and Palmer and Shanon were still chatting with the girl in the punk outfit. Amy chuckled. Miracle of miracles, Kate and Lisa were giggling together, and Palmer actually seemed interested in whatever the girl with orange hair was saying. Amy took a sip of her chocolate and glanced at the others. Little clusters of Alma girls were relaxing everywhere, sitting on benches, sprawled out on the grass, or standing around on the walks. Even the teachers seemed to have loosened up. On a bench next to Mr. Griffith, Miss Grayson was holding a purple balloon.

Amy stretched contentedly. It was great not to be standing in line for a change. And the weather was perfect! And tomorrow they'd be at Stratford-upon-Avon, the birthplace of Shakespeare and the home of Michael Oliver!

CHAPTER ELEVEN

———◆———

Right after breakfast the next day, the Alma girls took the bus to Stratford-upon-Avon. By ten thirty they were at Shakespeare's house. A guide showed them through the rooms, pointing out the beautiful antique furniture, including the dark, wooden cradle in the very bedroom where William Shakespeare was born.

"This is pretty neat," said Palmer. "Imagine— Shakespeare's mother must have rocked him in a cradle just like that!"

"It's awesome," said Lisa. "Just being here is giving me goose bumps."

"Enjoying yourselves?" Miss Grayson asked, coming up behind them.

"We sure are," said Lisa.

"This is a lot more interesting than I thought it would be," Palmer admitted as they walked outside to the small, carefully laid out garden. Amy and Shanon were already there with another group of girls and Mr. Griffith.

84

"How do I look?" Amy asked Shanon nervously. "Be perfectly honest."

"Fine," Shanon replied, looking up from a rosebush. "Isn't this wonderful? They've planted all the flowers mentioned in Shakespeare's plays here."

Amy glanced at the garden. "Yes, it's wonderful." She would have been more enthusiastic, but now that she was actually in Stratford-upon-Avon, she was more interested in Michael Oliver than in William Shakespeare.

"Are you sure I don't look too weird?" Amy asked. She was wearing a sleeveless black and white cotton jumper with a white blouse underneath and a tan trenchcoat.

"You look anything but weird," Shanon giggled. "In fact, you look unusually proper."

"That's what I mean," said Amy. "I can't believe it—on the day I'm going to meet Michael Oliver, they decide to enforce the dress code."

"It's probably because we're going to the theater," said Shanon, smiling.

Amy chuckled. "Oh, right, I almost forgot. I wish we could just skip the play, go straight to The Sandwich Board, and—"

Amy broke off abruptly as Kate came up to them. "Isn't this lovely?" Kate said with a dreamy expression. "I keep thinking about Romeo and Juliet. This is just the kind of garden Juliet must have had."

"I wish we were going to see *Romeo and Juliet* this afternoon," said Lisa.

"Don't worry," Kate said. "We're seeing *Hamlet!* You'll probably like it just as much as *Romeo and Juliet.*"

Amy nudged Kate. "When are we going to The Sandwich Board, before or after?"

Kate looked at her blankly. "Uh . . . I don't know."

Amy's heart started pounding. "You did ask Miss Grayson about it, didn't you?"

"I asked her, all right," Kate replied.

Amy swallowed. "And what did she say?"

"She said maybe," Kate answered.

Amy grinned with relief. "Great, that means we're going!"

"I wouldn't be so sure," Kate said doubtfully. "I told her how important it was to you. I even said I would go with you in a small group if—"

"You did that?" Amy exclaimed. "Wow! Thanks, Kate!"

"Well, it's the least I can do," Kate said, looking both pleased and embarrassed at the same time. "Anyway, I want to prove I'm not just a rule maniac."

"That's not what I think about you," Shanon said kindly.

"Oh, I know *you* don't," said Kate. "But I can't say the same for some other people—like your roommate," she added just as Mr. Griffith and some of the other girls joined them on the path.

"Have you and Miss Grayson decided whether we're going to The Sandwich Board?" Amy asked eagerly. "I think we should go before lunch!"

Mr. Griffith gave her a puzzled luck. "I'm afraid I don't understand."

"I only asked Miss Grayson about it," Kate cut in.

"I have a friend," Amy explained quickly, pulling out a map of Stratford-upon-Avon. "Actually, a friend of a friend of a friend," she went on. "He's a musician, and his father owns a restaurant on High Street."

Mr. Griffith examined the map. "According to this, that's not far away," he said.

Amy gasped. "Fantastic! I thought so! Stratford is a pretty small town. So, when can we go there? Lisa, Shanon, and Palmer want to go too. And Kate said she would go with us."

Mr. Griffith looked at his watch. "I don't know about this, Amy," he said doubtfully. "We're on a very tight schedule. Our matinee starts at one thirty."

Amy's heart began to race again. Here she was, in the very same town as Michael Oliver, and . . . it would be too awful if she couldn't even meet him!

"Please," she begged. "It'll only be for a few minutes."

Mr. Griffith looked thoughtful. "Who is this person? An old friend?"

"No, I told you," Amy said. "He's a friend of a friend of—"

"Ah, yes!" said Mr. Griffith, cutting her off. "So you said. Just out of curiosity, why is it so important that you see him?"

Amy stared at the teacher in confusion. She didn't quite know what to say. "Well . . . I've been writing to him," she began, "and . . . uh, my pen pal and I write songs, and this person. . . . It's hard to explain," she finished lamely. "I just really want to go there."

Mr. Griffith nodded. "Perhaps we might have tea there

. . . if time permits, that is. But now let's catch up with the others. We still have lots more to see before the play."

"Yippee!" said Amy as Mr. Griffith walked off toward Miss Grayson. "We're going."

"I don't know," said Shanon. "He said if time permits."

"But time will permit," said Amy. "It *has* to."

After completing the tour of Shakespeare's birthplace, the group took a short ride to the original home of Anne Hathaway, the girl who became Mrs. Shakespeare. Shanon, Lisa, and even Palmer marveled at the beauty of the quaint thatched-roofed farmhouse. But Amy waited outside on pins and needles. *Why don't they hurry up!* she thought impatiently. With every passing moment, her chances of getting to The Sandwich Board were fading. When Miss Grayson finally walked out of the farmhouse, Amy grabbed her arm.

"Please," she said, "have you thought about The Sandwich Board?"

"I understand how important it is to you," said Miss Grayson. "But I'm afraid we're running late at this point."

"Oh no," moaned Amy. "Can't we go right after we leave here?"

"We'll have to go straight to the theater after this," said Miss Grayson. "There's a park on the River Avon and we've brought box lunches for all you girls."

"I don't want a box lunch!" Amy balked. "The restaurant where I want to go isn't that far away from here. Mr. Griffith said so."

Miss Grayson sighed. "I'm really sorry," she said sympathetically. "What time were you hoping to meet your friend, anyway?"

"We never set a time," said Amy. "I was supposed to call him when I got here. If I don't get in touch with him soon, he'll think I'm not coming."

"Well, then," said Miss Grayson, making a decision, "you'd better call and say you won't be able to make it."

Amy drew in a breath. She felt like crying. "Really?" she asked weakly.

"Yes," Miss Grayson said. "There's a slim chance that if the show's not too long, we might still be able to stop at your friend's place for tea, but I can't promise. So to be on the safe side, you'd better tell him not to count on you." And then, looking at Amy's unhappy face, she added, "I really *am* sorry."

"That's okay," Amy said. "I realize it's a big favor to ask. After all, there are . . . a whole lot of us. If everybody wanted to go some special place, I guess it would be chaos."

Miss Grayson patted her shoulder. "Thanks for understanding."

Tears welled up in Amy's eyes as she walked to the souvenir section of the farmhouse in search of a telephone. *At least I've learned how to use a pay phone in England,* she thought glumly. She reached into her change purse, took out ten pence, and slowly dialed Michael Oliver's number.

"Michael Oliver here!" His voice sounded so upbeat and interesting. So musical!

"Hi," she said flatly. "It's Amy—"

"Thank goodness!" he said. "We've been hoping you'd ring up! Our spring break started today and we're all here early. There's even a real audience—"

"Just a minute," Amy interrupted. "I'm afraid I won't be coming."

Michael paused. "Ugh, what a downer. We'd cooked up a bit of a surprise for you."

"A surprise?"

"Yes. We've got a video set up for this afternoon's tea," he explained. "The group and I were hoping you'd make your English debut here."

Amy gulped. "My English debut?" she repeated.

"Yes," Michael continued. "We wanted you to sing your song for us. We think you're a fabulous performer. I've been practicing the melody so I could accompany you."

Amy felt the tears begin to overflow. "Oh, wow," she murmured, "I'm sorry. You went to so much trouble. Maybe the next time I come to England. . . ." Her voice trailed off. The last time she'd been here, she was five and now she was thirteen. By the time she made it again, she would probably be twenty.

"It really is a pity," Michael said. "Are you absolutely sure you can't make it?"

"We're going to see *Hamlet* this afternoon," Amy groaned.

"My father's restaurant is only a hop, skip, and a jump from the theater," he exclaimed. "Can't you get away from your group for just a moment?"

"No," said Amy. "I don't think so."

"The group will be so disappointed," he said.

There was a silence on the phone.

"I have to go now," Amy said in a dull voice. "They'll be

wondering where I am. We probably have to get back on the bus soon."

"Righto," Michael said. "Maybe next time. And if you compose any more songs in the future, please do let me know."

"I will," Amy promised. "Thanks again. Say hello to your sister Pamela."

Amy hung up the phone despondently and trudged into the souvenir shop. She caught sight of Palmer and Muffin eyeing a commemorative mug and Shanon at the cash register, buying a book on flowers. Off in a corner, Lisa was looking at postcards. Amy walked over to her.

"What's wrong?" Lisa asked right away. "You look bummed out."

"I am," Amy admitted. "I'm not going to be able to meet Michael Oliver. Miss Grayson said there's no time. I just talked to him."

"That's too bad," Lisa said softly.

"The dumbest part of all," Amy sputtered, "is that his father's restaurant is right near the theater. I'm going to be practically there and I still won't be able to see him. Not only that, I'm missing my English debut."

Lisa's eyes widened. "Your what?"

"They wanted me to sing," wailed Amy. "And they were even going to put me on videotape. For some reason, Michael Oliver and his group really like my singing."

"We all do," Lisa said loyally.

Suddenly, Amy felt like crying again. Fighting back tears, she ran for the bus. "If anybody wants to know where I am," she called back to Lisa, "I'm on the bus. . . ."

91

Some time later the rest of the Alma group boarded the bus, and before long they arrived at the park in front of the theater. The view of the River Avon was lovely. Lisa, Shanon, Palmer, and Amy sat on a bench near the water, each with a box lunch balanced on her lap.

"At least it hasn't rained," Shanon said, trying to sound cheerful.

"Right," Amy said expressionlessly.

"It just isn't fair!" Palmer fumed. "Something important like a debut and you have to miss it!"

"Miss Grayson did say there was a slim chance of going to The Sandwich Board for tea," Shanon volunteered.

"Fat chance," said Amy. "Ever since I asked to go, they've kept telling me maybe. I'm sure it won't be any different after we get out of the theater."

Lisa took out her map of Stratford-upon-Avon. "What street did you say the restaurant is on?" she asked.

"High Street," said Amy.

"That's so silly," exclaimed Lisa. "It's probably only five minutes from here!"

"So what?" Amy sighed. "We still can't go."

"I'm not so sure about that," Lisa muttered. She looked at Shanon. "Did you ever read *Hamlet?*"

"Sure," said Shanon. "I read the whole thing."

"Is it a long play?" asked Lisa.

Shanon nodded. "Very. It's also one of my favorites. There's a ghost in it."

Lisa's eyes gleamed mischievously. Just behind them was the theater. "I bet there are lots of scenes in it," she said. "Lots of chances for stepping out of the theater."

Amy's mouth dropped open. "Are you thinking what I think you're thinking?"

"I think so," Lisa said.

Shanon gasped. "You wouldn't!"

Palmer giggled. "Sounds like fun."

"I don't know," Amy said doubtfully.

Lisa shrugged. "Why not? It's just like sneaking into the kitchen at night back at Alma."

"I think it's a little more serious than that," said Shanon.

"So is Amy's English debut," Lisa argued. She turned to Amy. "So . . . what do you say?"

Amy looked at the map. What harm could it do to sneak out of *Hamlet*? High Street was just a few minutes away. No one would even know they were gone. Unless, of course, they got caught. . . .

"I think it's a great idea," Palmer chimed in. "And if Amy does decide to go, I'm going with her. I wouldn't miss her English debut for anything!"

"But what about Miss Grayson and Mr. Griffith?" Amy asked.

"It'll be dark in the theater," said Lisa. "They won't notice a thing."

"Bet you Kate will," Amy persisted.

"That's right," said Shanon. "Kate will definitely be keeping an eye on us. You know how seriously she takes her job as chaperone."

But Lisa wasn't about to give up. The wheels in her mind were spinning. "Don't worry about Kate," she said slyly. "I think I have an idea."

CHAPTER TWELVE

Shanon leaned forward in her seat. Her favorite part of the play was coming up. Hamlet was about to see the ghost! She almost jumped out of her skin when someone tapped her on the shoulder.

It was Palmer. "Come on!" she whispered. "It's time to go!"

Eyes still glued to the stage, Shanon slowly got to her feet. The four Foxes had managed to pick seats on the aisle in the last row of the block reserved for Alma. Three rows up and seven seats across sat Miss Grayson and Mr. Griffith. Feeling Palmer's tug again, Shanon tiptoed toward the back and out of the theater. The lobby was bright with daylight.

They quickly headed toward the ladies' room to meet Lisa and Amy.

"I hope this works," Shanon said anxiously.

"It'll be a breeze," Palmer assured her.

Inside the ladies' room, Lisa was slumped in a chair and

Kate and Amy were standing over her with concerned expressions on their faces.

"How are you doing, Lisa?" Palmer asked, trying to look as worried as the other girls.

"A little better," Lisa said pitifully. She touched her stomach. "It must have been something in those box lunches."

Kate wiped her brow and glanced toward the door nervously. "What's happening in *Hamlet?*" she asked Shanon.

"It's the ghost scene," Shanon replied.

"I'm missing one of the best scenes in the whole play," Kate said wistfully.

"Why don't you go back in?" Amy suggested. "There are three of us here. We'll take good care of Lisa."

"Are you sure you're not too sick?" Kate asked Lisa. "Because if you are, then I should stay with you."

"No, please don't do that," Lisa blurted out. "What I mean," she added in a calmer voice, "is that Shanon, Amy, and Palmer can take care of me."

"You're sure you don't want me to get Miss Grayson?" Kate went on. "Or maybe you should go to a doctor."

Lisa smiled wanly. "Really, it's not that serious. Just a little indigestion. But I would feel better," she added hastily, "if my friends could stay with me."

Kate eyed them suspiciously. "How come all three of you need to stay here?"

"Because we do everything together," Palmer said coolly.

Kate glanced toward the door again. "Well, just make

sure you come back to your seats as soon as Lisa feels better. And don't get into any trouble."

"Don't worry," Amy said as Kate hurried out of the lounge. "We won't!"

"It worked like a charm," Lisa giggled the minute the door closed behind Kate.

"You're a really good actress," said Palmer admiringly.

"So are you," said Lisa. "You really seemed concerned about me."

"Kate really *was* concerned," Shanon said quietly. "I feel bad about lying to her."

Amy patted Shanon's shoulder. "Listen, you don't have to come with me if you don't want to."

Shanon bit her lip. "Well . . . I do like *Hamlet*. . . ."

"But when are you going to get a chance to hear Amy sing in a real club again?" Lisa objected.

"That's right," said Palmer. "This is her English debut. Besides, don't you want to meet that cute guy, Michael Oliver?"

"Are you sure we won't get into trouble?" Shanon said cautiously.

"We will if we don't get out of here," Lisa replied. "We're wasting precious minutes." She turned to Amy. "Are you ready?"

"Ready as I'll ever be," Amy answered. She'd decided that whatever happened, going to The Sandwich Board would be worth it. Singing her song would be worth any kind of punishment. Besides, she thought, they weren't going to get caught anyway. The restaurant was practically next door to the theater.

The girls left the ladies' room, scurried across the lobby and through the big outside door.

"Everybody have your ticket stub so we can get back in?" Lisa asked hastily.

The other three girls nodded.

A cool breeze whipped at their skirts. The weather was changing.

"Hey," Palmer complained, shivering. "What happened to all that sunny weather?" To avoid arousing suspicion, they'd all left their coats in their seats.

Shanon looked up at the clouds. "Looks like it's about to start raining."

"That's impossible," Lisa said stubbornly. "It hasn't rained all week. Why should it start now?"

Amy chuckled nervously. "Because we're sneaking out. It'll be our punishment."

"Nobody is going to be punished," Lisa insisted. "Even if we do get caught, we'll probably just get a bunch of demerits."

Shanon sighed. "I hope you're right."

"Anyway," Palmer added, "the restaurant is just over on High Street. We can be there and back in ten minutes."

With a backward glance at the theater, the girls crossed the busy street. Using the map, they quickly found Sheep Street and turned onto High Street.

"I see it!" Lisa exclaimed, pointing to a quaint-looking restaurant with blue shutters. "It's up ahead!"

"The sign says The Sandwich Board, all right," Amy said excitedly.

Palmer looked at her watch and then at Shanon. "You

see, we haven't been gone more than five minutes."

"That's half of ten minutes," Shanon pointed out uneasily. "I just hope this is worth it."

"It will be," Amy promised. "I'll make sure it is." But when they reached the front of The Sandwich Board, Amy stopped abruptly. *What am I doing?* she thought in a panic. She'd been so worried about sneaking out to the restaurant, she'd almost forgotten that she was supposed to be *singing* here. She'd never sung for a big group before. So what if Michael Oliver and his group thought she had a good voice? *She* didn't! Right now she had to feel confident about herself. But all she felt was terrified.

Amy peered into the restaurant window cautiously. There were lots of people sitting at the tables, most of them teenagers.

"What are you waiting for?" Lisa urged. "Let's go in!"

"Uh . . . I don't know," said Amy. "My legs feel kind of wobbly."

"What does that have to do with it?" Palmer objected. "We've sneaked out of the theater for this. We've got to go in."

"This is your English debut," Lisa reminded her.

Amy's heart was pounding. "I . . . I'm not prepared," she stammered.

"I think you've got stage fright," Shanon said gently. "Don't worry. Your singing is wonderful. Everyone said so when you sang on the tape."

"That's right," Lisa agreed, opening the door to the restaurant and marching in. "All you have to do is what you do when you sing to us in the suite."

"Be brave," Palmer encouraged, squeezing in behind Lisa. "Just pretend you're singing to a pillow."

As soon as they were all inside, a tall boy with curly brown hair and a black beret strolled over.

"It's Michael Oliver," whispered Shanon. "I recognize him from his picture!"

Amy tried to compose herself.

"May I help you?" the tall boy asked with a friendly smile.

Palmer giggled. "Isn't his accent adorable?" she whispered to Shanon.

Lisa gave Amy a nudge forward. "This is your big chance," she said softly. "Don't blow it."

Amy forced a smile. "Hi, I'm uh . . . Amy Ho," she said, sticking her hand out.

"Amazing!" the boy said warmly. "Hey, gang!" he called out. "It's Amy Elizabeth." He shook her hand. "I'm Michael Oliver. So glad you could make it. And these are your friends?"

"Yes, we are," Lisa replied, stepping forward. "Could Amy sing her song as soon as possible? We're on sort of a tight schedule?"

"Righto!" said Michael Oliver.

Suddenly the whole room was buzzing with talk and laughter. Everyone there seemed to be looking at Amy. A girl she recognized as Michael's sister Pamela was standing next to a video camera.

"Okay, everyone!" Michael yelled, putting his hands up. "We're quite pleased to have a guest with us today from America. Pam and I have been playing her song lately at

99

some of the teas, so you may recognize it. I'm proud to present a really great singer—Amy Elizabeth!"

Palmer squealed and Lisa clapped her hands. "Isn't this exciting?" breathed Shanon. The three friends found seats at a nearby table, while Michael Oliver led Amy onto the platform in front of the room.

"What key?" Michael asked, sitting down at the piano.

Amy blinked. "Key?" She looked out at the audience. There were only about twenty people, but it seemed like a thousand. Their faces were swimming before her. Suddenly, Pamela turned on some bright camera lights.

"Hope that doesn't bother you," the English girl said politely.

"No, I'm fine," Amy lied, somehow managing to smile. Her mouth felt dry as cotton. Michael must have known, because he gave her a glass of water. She took a small swallow and put the glass down. Her stomach felt as if the bottom were falling out of it and her legs got even shakier.

Michael played a chord on the piano. "Is something wrong?" he asked softly.

"I . . . I don't think I can. . . ." Looking around helplessly, she caught sight of Lisa, Shanon, and Palmer. They were all beaming at her. They'd taken a big chance in coming here. How could she leave without even trying?

"Maybe you'd like guitar accompaniment," Pamela offered, leaving her position behind the camera.

"Yes, let's hear some strings," a deep voice suggested. Amy glanced in the direction of the voice, where a dark-haired man in a white apron was serving tea and sodas to the audience.

"That's my dad," Michael explained.

Beads of perspiration broke out on Amy's forehead. "I'll play for myself," she said, taking the guitar from one of the musicians. She smiled weakly. Did everybody else know how nervous she was? That any minute now, she felt like she would faint?

Amy played the first chord, and the audience quieted down. She remembered the first moment she'd thought of this music, the time when it was just inside her head. In spite of the tightness in her throat, her voice came out clear and true. "I was standing in the mist, when I thought I heard a hiss. . . ." Amy smiled. She could see the mist in her imagination, the face of the figure, the woman in blue handing out her card.

"It's Willa! Willameena the Bard.
Let me give you my card.
Yeah, it's written all in po-e-try!
ROCK OUT, WILLA! Willameena the Bard!"

Lisa nudged Shanon. "She's singing the song her way."

"She and John must have come to a different agreement," Shanon whispered. "Isn't she great?"

"Amazing!" Palmer said admiringly.

Amy's body filled with warmth and her voice got stronger and stronger. She hardly knew what she was singing, but the words came out automatically. The music and melody took over as the spirit of the raucous song filled the restaurant. "ROCK OUT, WILLA!" she cried. "Don't you know you're a star? I hook my light to you-oo!"

Amy let the guitar drop, and the audience burst into

applause. Her hair was soaked with perspiration. Something special had happened to her while she was singing. It was as if she'd been lifted off the planet and dropped down again; as if while she'd been singing she'd also been soaring. But all the same, she was glad it was over. She'd gotten through the song without a mistake!

"Fabulous!" Michael said, grabbing her as she came off the platform. "I love the changes!"

"What changes?" Amy asked, puzzled. "I—"

"We have to go!" Lisa interrupted.

"Yes, we'd better," Shanon said, beginning to worry again.

"Nice to meet you," Palmer said, batting her eyes at Michael Oliver. "By the way, do you know where I might buy some go-go boots?"

"Not now!" hissed Lisa.

Still dazed, Amy looked at Michael. "How can I ever thank you?" she asked happily.

"Just drop by the next time you're in England," the boy said, giving her a quick hug.

Palmer pulled at her arm. "Lisa's right. We'd really better get out of here."

Suddenly, Amy remembered Miss Grayson and *Hamlet* and gulped. "Yes, I guess we'd better. 'Bye, Pamela," she called to the girl behind the camera. " 'Bye Michael!" Then she and her suitemates dashed out the door.

"Wait!" Pamela called after them. "You forgot your videotape!" But the four girls were already halfway down the block.

"It's all right," Michael told his sister. "I've got her

address at school. We'll mail it to her. I really did like those changes. . . ."

Amy, Palmer, Shanon, and Lisa were now running at almost full speed. "Where are we?" Palmer asked, panting loudly.

"We should be there any minute!" Lisa replied breathlessly.

Shanon shot a smile at Amy. "You were sensational!"

"Was I?" Amy grinned. "I hardly knew what I was doing! It was like being in a dream!"

They stopped at a light, and Palmer felt a drop on her arm. "Oh, no," she said, "it's raining."

"Do you think they've noticed that we're missing?" Shanon asked with a worried frown.

Lisa gulped and looked at her watch. They'd been gone for thirty-five minutes! "They're probably all still watching the play," she said hopefully.

"Unless Kate came back to the bathroom," said Amy.

"She wouldn't have done that," said Lisa. "She was too into *Hamlet.*"

"But suppose she really did come back to the ladies' room?" said Shanon. "Suppose she had to *use* it?"

"Gosh," breathed Lisa. "I hadn't thought of that."

The sky suddenly darkened and it really started to rain, first in small drops and then in great torrents.

"Oh, no!" squealed Palmer. "We're going to get soaked."

Shanon groaned. "They'll *know* we've been outside if we turn up wet."

Lisa's heart started pounding. "Let's run for it!"

The girls dashed down High Street, missing the turn onto Sheep Street in their panic.

"Wait a minute!" gasped Amy. "Where's Sheep Street?" Everything looked different in the pouring rain.

"I think we ran past it," Lisa said frantically.

"Good grief," grumbled Palmer. Her thin blue skirt and sweater were drenched. "Now what do we do?"

Lisa let out a nervous laugh and licked some raindrops. "Head back toward the restaurant!" she instructed. "We'll hit Sheep Street sooner or later."

Giggling hysterically, they made an about-face and began to jog again.

"Actually, this is kind of fun," Shanon said giddily.

"It won't be much fun if we get caught," Amy reminded her.

"There it is!" Palmer squealed. "Sheep Street!"

"Thank goodness," said Lisa. "Let's hurry! We're almost back at the theater. Maybe no one's missed us yet."

As they were about to turn onto Sheep Street, they heard a very loud roar. It seemed to be coming from High Street, right near the restaurant.

"What was that?" Lisa asked, turning the corner.

"It sounded like someone yelling 'Stop!' " Shanon said breathlessly.

"Stop!" the voice rang out again. Palmer turned and saw someone a little ways behind them. It was a man in a big orange poncho, carrying a black umbrella that completely hid his face.

"I think there's someone following us," she said nervously.

Lisa glanced over her shoulder. "I think you're right." The man seemed to be coming right toward them.

"He looks scary with that umbrella over his face," Shanon gulped. "Sort of like a ghost."

"Don't be silly," said Amy, moving even faster anyway. Soaking wet and frightened, the four girls kept running. And so did the orange-ponchoed man.

"What does he want?" Lisa gasped. "Why is he following us?"

"Girls!" the man's voice rang out as he lowered the umbrella. "Amy! Lisa! Shanon! Palmer!"

The four girls stopped in their tracks and turned to face—Mr. Griffith.

"Thank heavens," Lisa sighed with relief.

"Boy," Palmer said, "that was close. We thought we were being followed by a stranger."

"Or a ghost," said Shanon.

Amy grinned. "And all the time it was you, Mr. Griffith."

The girls stood on the sidewalk, in the middle of the downpour. They began to giggle again, partially out of relief, but more out of embarrassment. Mr. Griffith, however, did not look amused. His green eyes were stormy.

Covering his face with the umbrella again, the young teacher stalked past them. "All right ladies," he said sternly, "let's go!"

"Uh-oh," Shanon groaned softly. "I think we're in for it now."

CHAPTER THIRTEEN

Dear Rob,

  As you can see, I have tragic news. Shanon, Palmer, Amy, and I got into big trouble. It happened while we were in London. Actually, it happened in a town near there called Stratford-upon-Avon. We all sneaked out of this theater for Amy's English debut. It's too long a story to go into now, but the result is that Mr. Griffith went to look for us and found us (not that we were really all that lost—I'm sure I would have been able to figure out the way back). And Miss Grayson was extremely mad. It was the first time I've ever seen her really angry. She has these incredible violet eyes and she was so mad that Shanon and I were sure we saw them change colors. The next day we still went shopping and to the Tower of London, but Miss Grayson didn't stop by to tuck us in on the airplane. And lots of our privileges have been taken away from us, including trips to town and social events. The VCR is still broken in our dorm, so that means there is virtually no entertainment. Worst of all, we had to go to Miss Pryn's office. That was scarier than seeing Halloween on the airplane. Miss Pryn has these little blue eyes that bore right through your whole being. She gave us the worst sentence possible—GROUNDED until further notice! I think the "until further notice" part is unjustly cruel. I was only trying to help Amy, and the restaurant was only a few minutes away from the theater, but I guess Miss Grayson and Mr. Griffith were really worried when they found out we weren't in the theater. To get to the very tragic point of this letter, I can't go to The Sixties with you! I guess you can still come, since Ardsley has been given a general invite. But Shanon, Amy, Palmer, and I have definitely been un-invited. Since we got back, I feel terrible. I have so much homework piled up, and I am always sneezing. Palmer and I got bad colds on account of being drenched that day in Stratford. What do you suppose "until further notice" means? Do you think I might be grounded all year? It is too painful to think about! I'm glad we are writing letters. They will mean even more to me now that I am almost like a prisoner!

Yours truly and dejectedly,
Lisa

107

Dear Mars,

I can hardly write to you, I feel so awful. So much about London was interesting, but I made a terrible mistake. I broke a major rule there. Along with my suitemates while we were in a town called Stratford-upon-Avon, I left the rest of the group without permission. It was awful. The school wrote to our parents, and my mom and dad were very disappointed in me. Believe me, I'll never do anything like that again. Mr. Griffith is the one who found us. We were actually lost for a few minutes—and in a foreign country! When we got back to Alma, Miss Pryn really let us have it! Lots of privileges are taken away from us for a while, one of them being all social activities. So, unfortunately, The Sixties is off limits. The punishment may sound harsh to you, but if Miss Grayson hadn't spoken up for us with Miss Pryn, it would have been much worse. We might even have been suspended!

Please feel free to go to The Sixties by yourself and have fun without me. I thought about you a lot while I was away. I even bought some English yarn to knit you a scarf. I also thought about you at the Tower of London. I was feeling very scared that day, since it was the day after we'd been caught by Mr. Griffith. And none of us knew what would happen to us when we got back to Alma. Did you know that in the olden days a lot of people in England were imprisoned in towers? Even people our age! A sixteen-year-old queen was once locked up there. Her name was Jane. It made me very sad to think about her. I couldn't help imagining what it would be like to be cooped up in a tower like that and how much I'd miss everyone.

Then we got back here, and Miss Pryn grounded us. I know it's not the same. We can still go to classes and eat at the dining hall, and I can still write you letters. But I am very disappointed not to get to see you. It's my fault and I'm sorry.

Sincerely,
Shanon

Dear Sam,

I have some crushing news. I will not be at The Sixties. Not only that, there was only one day of shopping in London. On the bright side, I did find some go-go boots, though now I'll have to wear them for some other occasion. I found them in an old-fashioned clothing store. At first when I asked for some antique shoes from the sixties, the storekeeper didn't know which sixties I was talking about—eighteen sixty or nineteen sixty! Then we got it straight, and she actually had the shoes I wanted. They are short and white and have fringe on them in case you're interested. I will close now. By the way, were you planning to come to the dance? The last time you wrote, you were waiting to find out whether you were going to play at Brier Hall. I hope you're not. Please write soon.

Fondly,
Palmer

Dear John,

A major drag. We are grounded. Sorry, but I won't be able to see you here at the dance. But wait until you hear what happened in England. I met Michael Oliver! He was

109

totally rad, and so was his sister. I got to sing our song "Young Willie." Shanon, Palmer, and Lisa said I was great! I don't know. Boy, was I scared! I was seeing stars! I think it might be a while before I sing in front of people in person again. Michael Oliver sent me a cool letter in which he said I was the find of the twenty-first century! Pretty nice. He and Pam also sent me a videotape of myself performing. Unfortunately, the VCR in Fox Hall isn't fixed yet, so I can't even watch it. So I am sending it with this letter to you. I hope you like it. I am sad not to be seeing you soon, but—

See you sometime in the future!
Amy

CHAPTER FOURTEEN

Dear Lisa,

I was looking forward to seeing you a lot. I had even gotten some old clothes from my father for a costume. There's talk of something coming up at Ardsley sometime in the near future, however, to which we can invite "chicks." Ha-ha. See, I was even practicing my sixties lingo. Enclosed is a piece of hard candy. Consider it a prison treat and think of me.

I'll wait for you!
Rob

Dear Shanon,

I was very disappointed when I got your letter. If you broke a rule, I'm sure it was for a good cause. I hope Miss Pryn won't keep you grounded forever, though. I was all set to see you at the dance, since I had been missing you. Send me your ghost story. The Tower of London sounds too weird. Talk about ghosts, I'll bet you anything that *there are a few of them in that place. Keep your chin up.*

Your pal,
Mars

Dear Palmer,
The Fantasy and I didn't get the gig at Brier Hall, so I would have made it to the dance at Alma. I'm sorry I won't get to see you. Hope you're not grounded for too much longer. Congratulations on finding those boots.

Sincerely,
Sam O'Leary

Dear Amy,
My feelings were very hurt by the tape you sent me. A better word might be wounded *or maybe* perplexed. *Your behavior is weird, but I guess you and Michael Oliver don't care what I think. Maybe he can be your new pen pal. I'm sure you will find that much more interesting.*

John

P.S. My father's old jacket that he wore at Woodstock arrived in the mail the same day that your videotape did. I was going to wear it to the dance. It is ironic!

"I don't get it!" said Amy. "I thought John would be glad I'd sung our song!"

Palmer sneezed. "Maybe we should make some hot tea," Lisa sniffed, passing her the tissue box.

Shanon got out her teapot and heating coil. "I can't understand John's attitude either," she said to Amy.

"Sounds like he's jealous," volunteered Lisa.

"Or maybe he likes you so much he's being mean to

you," Shanon reasoned, "just like Hamlet was to Ophelia."

Palmer pulled her bathrobe closer. "What does it matter anyway? You've got this new pen pal, Michael Oliver. He's a lot cuter than John!"

"He is *not* cuter than John!" Amy said hotly. "And Michael Oliver isn't my pen pal! The pen pal I want is John Adams!" She shook her head in frustration. "If only I knew what he was so upset about. Maybe he thought I did an awful job singing the song, and that's why he's mad at me."

"But you did a great job!" Lisa argued, slowly unwrapping the piece of hard candy. "Maybe I should save this candy Rob gave me for tonight," she said wistfully, wrapping it up again.

Shanon passed out some teacups. "Lisa is right," she told Amy. "You have nothing to be ashamed of as far as your performance in England. Perhaps we should have thought twice before sneaking out that way, but your singing—"

"Her singing was dynamite!" chimed in Palmer. "You know how I know?"

"How?" Amy asked her.

Palmer put some honey in her tea and licked the spoon. "I guess I can tell you now. The fact is, I never liked that song, 'Willameena.' Nothing against you—I've just always hated the name. But when you sang it at The Sandwich Board—"

"Hold on," said Amy. "You mean when I sang 'Young Willie.' "

"Same difference." Palmer shrugged.

"It is *not* the same difference," Amy insisted. "John and I had a terrible fight over those lyrics. They were similar, but not the same."

Shanon sipped her tea. "But in the end, he agreed that 'Willameena' was better, right?"

"He must have," said Lisa. "Otherwise Amy wouldn't have sung it that way when we were in England."

"I don't understand!" Amy exclaimed. "What are you talking about? I did not sing a song about an old lady named Willameena! I sang a song about a young man named Willie!"

"No, you didn't!" Palmer repeated.

"You sang the song your way," Lisa added. "Don't you remember?"

Amy's eyes widened. "Oh, no! How *could* I have? Are you absolutely sure about this?"

Shanon nodded. "Positively."

"My gosh!" said Amy. "No wonder John is angry! He must think I stabbed him in the back on purpose! He'll probably never—"

Amy broke off as the door to the suite popped open and Brenda Smith walked in. "Just wanted to thank you for your postcard," Brenda said cheerfully. She jiggled her foot. "Look, no more broken toe!"

"That's great," said Lisa.

"Isn't it?" Brenda grinned happily. "Now I can dance at The Sixties. Look—some of us got together and learned a dance called the frug last week!" Giggling, she shimmied across the floor.

Lisa looked away and Shanon made herself busy with

114

the teapot. "Nice dance," Palmer said flatly. "Sorry we can't join you."

Brenda stopped herself. "Oops! I'm sorry. For a minute I forgot you guys aren't going."

"There'll be other dances," Lisa said bravely.

"It really is a pity," Brenda said. "Have you told your pen pals yet?"

"We wrote to them," said Shanon. "They may still come, even though we won't be there."

"John, too?" Brenda asked curiously.

Amy gulped. "I think we can definitely count him out. It'll be a purple day in December before John Adams sets foot at Alma Stephens again."

"That's terrible," Brenda moaned.

There was an uncomfortable silence, and then Amy stepped out of the room.

Lisa looked at Brenda and cleared her throat. "Well . . . I should be hitting my Latin book."

"I've got biology to study," Palmer said, tapping her slipper.

Shanon finished off the tea without a word.

"I can take a hint," Brenda said. "Guess you guys don't need me around when you're suffering. I just wanted you to know how sorry I am about your being grounded. I hope it doesn't extend so long that you miss the movie."

Lisa lifted an eyebrow. "Miss what movie?"

"There's a big town trip planned," Brenda said enthusiastically, "and the whole school is—"

"Don't tell us anymore!" Lisa demanded. "It's too painful!"

"Okay," Brenda said, slipping out the door. "See you later!"

Palmer groaned. "She sure knows how to rub it in!"

"I'm sure Brenda meant well," said Shanon.

Lisa looked around. "Where's Amy?"

"Here I am," a mournful voice said from the bedroom doorway. "I just wanted you guys to know how sorry I am," she sniffed, tears streaming down her face. "I hate to cry, but I just can't help it. I should never have gotten you all involved in this mess."

"It's not your fault," said Shanon.

"Yes, it is," Amy insisted, grabbing a tissue and wiping her eyes. "If it hadn't been for my English debut, the three of you would be going to the dance."

"We made the decision ourselves," Lisa said, stifling a sneeze. "Rats, I wish this cold would get better!"

"Not only that," Amy moaned, starting to cry again, "but I've hurt John's feelings and now he hates me!"

"Stop," Shanon whimpered. "You'll make me cry, too." She put her arm around Amy.

"I feel like crying myself," Palmer moaned soulfully. "To think that Sam is actually coming to the dance at Alma and I won't be there." As she dropped dramatically down on the pink loveseat, Lisa suddenly started to giggle.

"This is ridiculous!" Lisa said. "Look at us—we're all sniffling like babies! Let's stop feeling so sorry for ourselves and do something that will make us feel better."

"Good idea," sighed Palmer. "I think I'll take a long hot bubble bath."

"I'm going to get a soda out of the machine downstairs," said Lisa. "Anyone want one?"

"Yes!" Palmer called, walking into the bedroom. "Bring me a diet cola!"

Amy looked at Shanon. "What about you?"

"I don't know," Shanon said. "Maybe I'll work on my ghost story or write to Mars." Before walking away, she gave her friend a pat on the shoulder. "Try not to feel bad about us . . . really."

"Thanks," Amy said, crossing to the desk. "I need to write a letter, too," she said quietly. "If only I can figure out what to say."

She sat for a moment and thought. Then, tearing a page out of her notebook, she started to write:

Dear John,
 I don't know what happened when I was singing—

Dear John,
 I honestly thought that Willameena the Bard was dead, but—

Dear John,
 The fact that you are my friend means a lot. I didn't know how much until—

Dear John,
 I'm sure you will find this hard to imagine, but I didn't even realize—

Dear John,
 I don't want to lose your friendship. Please let me explain—

Amy sighed and put her pen down. Then, one by one, she crumpled up the unfinished letters and tossed them into the wastebasket. "What's the use?" she muttered sadly. "He'd never believe me!"

CHAPTER FIFTEEN

"What a perfect night!" Shanon said, gazing dreamily out of the window at the star-studded sky. On the other end of the quadrangle, the brightly lit gym glowed like an unattainable jewel.

"Come on," Palmer demanded. "I thought we were playing a game of Hearts."

"I'll deal the cards," Amy volunteered. She shot a quick look at Shanon. "Can you see anything?"

"I think I see Kate leaving," Shanon replied, still looking out the window. "She showed me her costume earlier."

Palmer giggled. "Kate and her costumes! I'm sorry to have missed it. I hope she didn't dress up as a refrigerator."

"That's what she wore at Halloween," Shanon said defensively. "Tonight she has something very sixties— some embroidered jeans and a blue work shirt."

"I'm wearing jeans now," Amy said, shuffling the cards. "That's not much of a costume."

"It is for Kate," Shanon said, moving reluctantly away

from the window. "I don't think she's ever worn a pair of jeans in her life. She had to borrow them."

Amy dealt the cards, and Palmer tossed her head and sighed. Shanon finally joined them, sitting cross-legged on the floor.

"I ordered pizza from Figaro's," Amy muttered, examining the cards in her hand. "We'll have to listen for the za-wagon," she said, using their special name for Figaro's delivery van. "The whole dorm will probably be empty tonight, except for us."

Palmer glanced at one of the bedrooms. "What's Lisa doing in there?" she asked Shanon.

"I suppose she's still asleep," Shanon replied. "She's really disappointed about missing the dance tonight. She doesn't want anyone to disturb her."

"Lisa's not asleep," said Amy. "I just heard her moving around in there."

"Maybe we can get her to go down and check for the pizza man," Palmer said lazily. She threw her cards down. "I'm not in the mood for Hearts after all."

The bedroom door opened suddenly, and Lisa walked slowly into the sitting room. She was wearing an orange mini-dress, beads, and a headband. Her hair hung down perfectly straight as if it had been ironed.

"Wow!" Amy exclaimed. "Look at you!"

Lisa stretched out her arms and kept moving forward.

"Oh, my gosh!" whispered Shanon. "She's sleepwalking!"

"No, she isn't," said Palmer. "She's just kidding us! Okay, Lisa, that's enough now!"

Lisa continued to circle the room as if in a trance. "I—am—still—asleep," she said in an exaggerated monotone. "I—am—going—to—The Sixties!" And she started for the door that led to the corridor.

Amy jumped up. "No, you're not!" she said, laughing.

"Catch her!" said Palmer. "If *we* can't go, *she* can't go either!"

Palmer and Amy grabbed Lisa's arms and pulled her back in. "Gotcha!" Lisa said with a grin.

"You almost did have me fooled," Shanon admitted. "Almost!"

Lisa plopped down on the loveseat. "I just couldn't resist putting on my costume," she sighed. "Then I had this idea of pretending to sleepwalk over to the gym."

"Don't you dare!" said Amy. "We're in enough trouble already!"

"I know," Lisa said. "All I would do is peek in the window. Just to see if Rob's there."

"I'd like to know if Mars is there, too," Shanon said wistfully.

"I know what!" suggested Amy. "Let's all get into our costumes! We've got a za coming. Why shouldn't we have our own Sixties Party?"

"Did they eat pizza then?" Palmer wanted to know.

Lisa snorted. "You've got to be kidding! We're talking about the nineteen sixties, remember? Not the fifteen sixties!"

"How should I know if pizza was invented then?" Palmer snapped. "I wasn't even born in the nineteen sixties! Maybe pizza was invented in the nineteen seventies!

They just recently invented Japanese sushi, you know!"

"Tell me you're kidding," Lisa said. "Everyone knows that—"

Amy put her hands over her ears. "Could we please not argue?"

"I agree," said Shanon. "Especially not tonight."

They all drifted slowly toward the window. By now the dance would have started. "I wish we could hear the music," Lisa said.

"It's too far away," Amy told her.

"I wonder if Sam is there," Palmer mused.

Lisa closed the window. "Who knows? Maybe Sam and The Unknowns decided to go to Brier Hall. Their dance is tonight, too, don't forget."

"If John had to choose, I'm sure he went to Brier Hall," sighed Amy, walking away. "I'm going to put on my costume."

Lisa went downstairs to check for the delivery van, and minutes later she returned with a piping-hot pizza. While she was gone, Shanon changed into a long dress with bright purple flowers and pinned a paper rose behind one ear. Palmer put on a blue-flowered headband, short white skirt, tie dyed T-shirt, and her go-go boots. And finally Amy came out of her room in a black leather vest and skirt.

"I thought you were wearing a costume," Shanon said.

Amy shrugged. "Black leather is classic. They wore it back then, too. Anyway, I have on feather earrings. They're very sixties."

The girls sat on the floor and ate their pizza while Shanon read them the tail end of her ghost story. . . .

"The room was still and dark. There was not a noise in the house, not even the clock. A shiver ran up the heroine's spine. Was she really alone? Was there not a ghost traveling abroad from out of the attic? Suddenly, there was a scratching noise. The heroine started! What could it be? She was supposed to be totally alone in the house, but she'd definitely heard something—"

"Shh!" Lisa cut in. "I just heard something."

"For real?" said Palmer, putting her pizza down.

The four girls listened.

"It must be your imagination," Amy said. "Shanon's story is scarier than she thinks it is."

"Thanks a lot," said Shanon. "We're almost at the end. Should I keep reading?"

Suddenly, there was a strange noise at the window.

"There it is again!" Lisa exclaimed. "It sounded like scratching!"

"How could it be scratching?" Amy argued. "We're on the third floor."

"Maybe it's a bird," Shanon suggested.

Palmer rolled her eyes. "A bird? At this time of night?"

There was an even louder noise at the window. This time it was more recognizable.

"Somebody's throwing stones at our window!" declared Amy.

Shanon drew in a breath. "Listen. . . . I hear voices."

"Someone's singing," Palmer said, drawing closer.

Lisa got up and cautiously opened the window. The voices swelled.

"Oh, my gosh!" gasped Lisa.

Palmer ran over. "What is it?"

"It's The Unknown!" she exclaimed. "They're down there singing!"

"Sam is there, too!" squealed Palmer. "I see him! Look!"

Shanon and Amy ran over.

"Is Mars there?" Shanon asked, squeezing in front of her friends.

Amy peered over Lisa's shoulder. "What about John?"

"I don't see him," said Lisa. "But the other three are there."

"They're serenading us!" Palmer exclaimed.

"How romantic!" said Shanon.

"Quiet for a minute," said Amy. "What's that they're singing?"

The four girls strained to hear the words of the boys' song. Sam O'Leary's mellow voice was in the lead and he was playing guitar. "It's Willa, Willameena the Bard. . . ."

Lisa laughed. "It's Amy's song! Wow!"

"That's nice," Amy said quietly. "I guess John must have played them the tape."

"It sounds great with Sam singing it!" Palmer said.

Lisa stuck her head out the window and waved, while Shanon and Palmer crowded in beside her. Retreating to a corner of the room, Amy picked at some cold pizza.

"Nice singing, you guys!" Lisa called gaily.

"Thought we'd give the prisoners a serenade!" a boy's voice answered.

"That was Rob!" cried Lisa. "I wish we could see them better!"

"Where's Mars going?" Shanon asked as her pen pal disappeared for a moment.

Lisa started to giggle as Mars came back with a ladder. "Oh, my goodness! They're going to come up!"

Shanon turned pale. "They can't!"

"I know they can't," Lisa said shrilly, "but how are we going to stop them?"

"Too late!" shrieked Palmer as Rob's face appeared at the window.

"Hi," he said awkwardly. "Guess you're surprised to see me."

Lisa laughed and blushed. "Sort of."

Rob blushed too as he handed her a beat-up-looking napkin with something wrapped inside it. "Here," he said. "Have some cake."

Lisa giggled. "Thank you."

"Didn't . . . uh, didn't want you to miss anything," he stammered with a smile. "They're serving it at the party."

"Hey, Williams!" a voice called from the ground. "Let me up there!"

"Oops," said Rob, "I'd better go. I'd demonstrate my frugging for you on this ladder," he chuckled, "but I wouldn't want to have an accident."

"No, don't do that," said Lisa as he climbed down swiftly. "Be careful."

"How do you like my sixties shirt?" he asked.

"It's great!" Lisa called back, squinting to see the bold patchwork pattern. "Very vintage!"

Palmer was breathing down Lisa's neck. "I wonder who's coming up next. I hope it's Sam!"

But Mars Martinez's face was next to appear at the window. Down on the ground someone was still singing "Willameena."

Seeing Mars's face, Shanon stepped forward shyly.

"Hi," he said with a grin. "Am I in the presence of a genuine flower child?"

Shanon self-consciously touched the flower behind her ear. "Well, back then a lot of people wore flowers."

"They should bring back the tradition," said Mars. "You look great that way."

Shanon stared at him, tongue-tied. *Mars must have the biggest brown eyes in the whole world!* she thought. "We, um, thought you guys might be at Brier Hall tonight," she finally managed to say.

"No," Mars chuckled softly, "we're definitely Alma men!" Knocking on the window, he waved at Amy. "All of us!"

"Nice to see you!" Amy called weakly. "How's the dance going?"

"Dull and boring without you!" Mars called back.

He reached in and grabbed Shanon's hand for a minute. "I guess I'd better not hog the whole prison visit. O'Leary still wants to get a peek at Palmer."

"Okay," Shanon said, stepping back from the window with a sigh.

"Did you say that Sam wants to see me?" Palmer clamored as Mars went down and Sam O'Leary came up. On the ground someone was still making music.

"Aren't they cute?" Lisa said, collapsing onto the couch.

"They sure do love Amy's song," said Shanon. "Somebody's still singing it," she added as Sam O'Leary's handsome face appeared at the window.

"Just thought I'd pop by!" Sam said, flashing Palmer a smile.

Palmer tossed her head. "Nice to see you." She stared at Sam's reddish-blond hair. It was almost as long as hers. "You grew your hair even longer!" she exclaimed. "Is that for the dance?"

"No, for myself," Sam answered. "Look! I've even got an earring!"

Palmer blushed. She'd never known a boy with an earring before. She was sure her mother would never approve. But, of course, Sam *was* an entertainer.

"I loved your singing just a minute ago," Palmer said. "I'm glad you came to Alma instead of Brier Hall."

"I was hoping to catch sight of you some way," Sam said sweetly. "But it was Mars who figured out how."

"Wait a minute," Shanon said from the other side of the room. "If Sam's on the ladder talking to Palmer, who is that singing? Mars is on the ground, holding the ladder."

"It can't be Rob," said Lisa. "His voice is still changing. Whoever is singing has a deep voice."

"Got to go!" Sam was saying to Palmer. "Don't want to get you girls into any more trouble."

"That's the truth," Palmer giggled.

"Don't forget to put the ladder away!" Lisa instructed.

"Not yet!" Sam called, disappearing. "There's one more Unknown making a visit!"

Amy stood up. Outside the singing had stopped. "Another Unknown?"

127

"It's not Rob," said Lisa. "He already came up."

"It's not Mars," piped up Shanon.

"And Sam O'Leary isn't an Unknown," Palmer reminded her.

Her heart pounding loudly, Amy crossed to the window. There was only one person it could be. And, sure enough, perched on the top of the ladder in a worn denim jacket—was John!

"Wow!" Amy murmured, feeling bewildered.

John's brown eyes twinkled. *"Like* wow!" he said. "That's sixties lingo."

Amy shook her head and swallowed. She didn't know what to think. "I . . . didn't see you before . . . on the ground."

"I was hiding behind a tree," John confessed. In the starlight, his red hair looked darker. "I was scared to say hello. Thought you might punch me out."

"Me? But you're the one who's mad. . . ." Her voice trailed off.

John gulped. "You look cool. The dance is insipid without you."

Amy's eyes gleamed. "I don't understand. I thought that after Willa—"

"I changed my mind," John cut her off. "I'll write to you . . . all about it."

Amy's whole body flooded with warmth. "Gee. . . ."

"Wow. . . ." said John, smiling broadly.

"Quite a conversation they're having," whispered Lisa with a giggle. "Gee . . . wow . . . wow . . . gee!"

Shanon tiptoed to the window. "We'd better call it

quits," she warned. "Hi, John," she added politely.

Amy looked at John. "Shanon's right. Even though we're not technically breaking a rule, since you're still outside and we didn't give you the ladder—"

John nodded understandingly. "The powers that be might not like it anyway?"

Amy grinned. "Something like that."

"Say no more," John said, starting down the ladder. "How do you like my father's Woodstock jacket?" he asked, looking back up at her.

"It's great!" Amy replied, craning her neck.

He stopped in the middle for a moment and gazed into her eyes, as if there was something more he wanted to say. "Like . . . wow," he said. "What can I say?"

Amy grinned. *"Like* . . . gee," she joked, "maybe nothing."

John laughed and jumped to the ground. Then he waved up at the window. "Bye-bye, I'll write!"

CHAPTER SIXTEEN

"So, now, young ladies," said Miss Grayson, "I hope we all understand one another."

"Yes, we understand," Lisa said humbly.

"I'll never pull a stunt like that again," Shanon vowed.

"Me neither," Palmer said, sounding truly sorry.

Miss Grayson looked at Amy. "What about you? No more English debuts?"

"No, ma'am," Amy replied earnestly. "Truthfully, I was very scared when we got lost."

"I was too," Lisa confessed. "I'm glad Mr. Griffith came after us."

Miss Grayson's eyes twinkled. "Really?"

Lisa smothered a giggle. "Sort of. Actually, he was scarier than getting lost."

"Yes," Shanon chimed in. "He looked like the headless horseman with his face all covered by that umbrella."

Miss Grayson suppressed a smile. "I'll let you four go," she said. The living room of her cozy little apartment was filled with the sweet smell of flowers.

"What pretty freesia," Shanon said, gathering up her books.

Miss Grayson tried to hide a grin as she glanced at the vase of yellow flowers on her desk.

"They are nice," Lisa chimed in, sniffing the air. "Did you pick them around here?"

The French teacher's violet eyes glistened. "No, they were a gift," she replied simply. Then she put her arms around the girls' shoulders. "So, no more sneaking off without permission? Either here or anywhere else?"

"Never again," Amy said, hugging her.

Miss Grayson patted Shanon's head and then Lisa's, and gave a big smile to Palmer. "You girls are very important. We have to take care of you," she said, walking them to the door.

"She is so nice," said Lisa when the girls were alone in the hallway.

"I bet Dan Griffith sent those flowers," Palmer said slyly.

Shanon nodded. "Probably. Things must really be serious between those two."

"They're both so nice," said Amy. "Too bad we bummed them out by breaking a rule."

"Yes," said Lisa, "I've learned my lesson. I'll never break another rule again."

"Even the one about not raiding the refrigerator?" Palmer challenged.

"Well, maybe that one," Lisa hedged. "Everybody breaks that."

Amy took the stairs two by two, and the other three girls followed.

"I feel like a pillow fight!" Amy called back playfully.

"Oh, no," cried Lisa. "Who are you mad at this time?"

"Nobody," Amy said, smiling over her shoulder. "I mean a *real* pillow fight! Last one in the room is a stinking sneaker!"

Shanon, Palmer, and Lisa all squealed and chased Amy into the suite. Palmer was the last inside.

"Stinking sneaker!" Amy cried, aiming a pillow at her.

"Don't you dare hit me!" Palmer laughed. "I don't want to get my hair all messed up!"

"Isn't that a shame!" Lisa said, popping her from behind with a sofa cushion.

They charged into Lisa and Shanon's room, throwing every pillow in sight. Then they fell on the floor, giggling happily.

"Look at all these feathers!" Shanon said, noting how one of the pillows had come unstuffed.

"It looks like a chicken house!" said Lisa.

"Or as they said in the sixties," Amy joked, "a 'chick' house!"

Palmer laughed and fluffed up her hair. "I wonder when we'll get to see the boys again."

"I can't wait," sighed Lisa. "It was so exciting when they climbed the ladder the night of the dance."

Amy reached into her pocket. "Guess what? John wrote me a letter."

"Let's hear it," Shanon said, rolling onto her stomach.

Dear Amy,

   What I really wanted to say when I saw you is that I am sorry for being so selfish. I'm afraid I have a big ego, and all I could see when I saw that tape was that you had ditched my words to the song. I was also angry that you were getting to be friends with Michael Oliver and his sister. I wanted to be in on that too. It's hard to admit it when somebody else does something better than you, but I've got to admit that in the case of our song, you made it better. I guess it's because you have such a good sense of humor. Mars and Rob rib me a lot because they say I'm too serious. I hope you don't think so—or that I'm too uptight or have a swelled head. I do not think you are conceited or weird. Instead, I think you are a neat person. And the only thing left for me to say is, I love you, Willameena.

John

   "I love you, Willameena!" Lisa said, her eyes lighting up. "What do you think that means?"

   Amy shrugged. "How should I know? Something nice."

   "I think it means he loves *you!*" Palmer suggested.

   "Don't be silly!" Amy said, grabbing a pillow. "It's just an apology. I had already written him that I didn't change the words at The Sandwich Board on purpose. So he knows I wasn't actually trying to hurt his feelings, even though I did."

   Shanon blew out a breath. "Wow, it sure is complicated."

   "I agree," said Lisa. "Those pen pals of ours can be hard to figure out sometimes."

"But it's all cleared up now," Amy said cheerfully. "I wouldn't care now what words he put in our song!"

Palmer looked at her quizzically. "How come you changed your mind about it? That song was so important."

"Willameena, Pillameena!" Amy giggled. "It's not as important as—"

"John?" teased Lisa.

Amy blushed. "Yeah, okay. It's not as important as getting along with John. I like him as a pen pal. Anyway, we're on to other things now. There's more to life than music, you know." She opened a pack of bubble gum and passed it around.

"I wonder how long we'll have our pen pals," Shanon said philosophically.

"Maybe forever," Lisa said. "Maybe until we're in college."

"Maybe until we're as old as Willameena," Palmer laughed. She jumped up and looked in the mirror. "I hope I never get old, though."

"Why not?" Lisa said, chewing her bubble gum. "Old people are fun. My grandmother is. Gammy hangs out with all her old buddies."

"Wow," said Shanon, "that's neat."

Amy's eyes gleamed. "I think so, too. When I'm old, I definitely still want to hang out with my friends."

Lisa laughed. "Maybe *we'll* still be hanging out together."

Palmer giggled. "But not still here at Alma Stephens."

"I guess not," Shanon said wistfully. She looked around and smiled. "But even when we're ninety, there's one thing I hope will never change."

"What's that?" said Amy, tugging her friend's braid.

Shanon smiled. "I hope that forever and ever, even when we're old, we'll still be the Foxes!"

They sat in a circle on the floor and blew bubbles.

Something to write home about . . .
two new Pen Pals stories!

In Book 7, Shanon's feelings are hurt when she realizes that everyone thinks she is shy and timid. To prove that she's got as much leadership potential as anyone, she decides to run for the Alma Stephens Student Council. But when she finds out that her main competition is her outgoing best friend, Lisa, she begins to have second thoughts.

Here's a scene from Pen Pals #7: HANDLE WITH CARE

As she brushed her teeth in the bathroom that night, Shanon stared at her reflection in the mirror. What are you doing, she asked herself. Running against somebody quiet like Muffin Talbot was one thing. But how could she possibly compete against someone as popular as Lisa? Lisa would undoubtedly win the election with one hand tied behind her back. And, to be honest, even Shanon believed that outspoken Lisa would probably be a better dorm rep than someone like herself. Besides, Lisa was her friend! Maybe she should just drop out of the race right now and become Lisa's campaign manager instead.

Shanon quickly undid her braid, brushed out her hair, and turned around to leave the bathroom. As she walked out the door, she almost crashed into Lisa, who was just coming in.

"Hi, Shanon," Lisa said.

"Hi," Shanon answered shyly.

For a few seconds, the two girls stood outside the bathroom door, looking at each other. Then Lisa smiled.

"I guess we took each other by surprise at the meeting tonight, didn't we?"

"I guess we did," Shanon said. "I'm sorry I didn't tell you I was running for dorm rep. I don't know why I didn't—I guess the subject just never came up, or something. But I want you to know I wouldn't have done it if I'd had any idea you were going to be running, too! In fact, I've just decided—"

"Well, of course I feel the same way," Lisa broke in. "Come back in the bathroom with me and maybe we can figure out what to do."

With a sudden feeling of relief, Shanon followed her roommate back into the bathroom and stood by the sink while Lisa carefully examined an almost invisible splotch on her cheek. "I'm really sorry about all of this," Lisa said after a minute. "And I'd be even sorrier if you got your feelings hurt in the election. I mean I'm sure you have loads of good ideas for things you'd want to do as dorm rep, but you know how kids are. They're not going to pay a whole lot of attention to the actual issues and. . . ." Her voice trailed off as she caught sight of Shanon's face reflected in the mirror.

"What exactly are you trying to say, Lisa?" Shanon asked.

"Oh, nothing really. Just that I thought you might have changed your mind about being in the election now that you know who you'd be running against. I mean, I'm sure Muffin Talbot is having second thoughts. You know how she is. She's kind of—"

"Kind of quiet? Kind of shy? Kind of like me?" Shanon asked.

Lisa turned away from the mirror and stared at her friend. Shanon's face was flushed with embarrassment or anger—Lisa wasn't sure which. But her soft hazel eyes were definitely filled with tears.

All at once, Lisa felt just awful. "I didn't mean that at all," she began. "I just don't want you to get hurt, that's all."

"What you meant was that you think you're such a sure bet to win by a landslide that Muffin and I might as well not even bother to run, isn't that it?"

Lisa started putting toothpaste on her toothbrush. "Well, you do have to admit I know a lot more people in the dorm than you do, Shanon."

"B-but that's not what this election is about!" Shanon stammered. "It's about who'd make the better dorm rep! It's about electing somebody with good ideas who'd be a good leader! And I just want you to know that you're not the only person in the world who fits that d-description!"

139

There's no way Shanon is going to drop out of the election now. Can Amy and Palmer keep the peace in suite 3-D? No matter who wins, will Shanon and Lisa's friendship ever be the same?

PEN PALS #8: SEALED WITH A KISS

When the Ardsley and Alma drama departments join forces to produce a rock musical, Lisa and Amy audition just for fun. Lisa lands a place in the chorus, but Amy gets a leading role. Lisa can't help feeling a little jealous, especially when her pen pal Rob also gets a leading role—opposite Amy. To make matters worse, the director wants Rob and Amy to kiss! Amy is so caught up in the play that she doesn't notice Lisa's jealousy—at first. And when she finally does notice, the damage has already been done! Is it too late to save their friendship?

P.S. Have you missed any *Pen Pals?* Catch up now!

PEN PALS #1: BOYS WANTED!

Suitemates Lisa, Shanon, Amy, and Palmer love the Alma Stephens School for Girls. There's only one problem—no boys! So the girls put an ad in the newspaper of the nearby Ardsley Academy for Boys asking for male pen pals. Soon their mailboxes are flooded with letters and photos from Ardsley boys, but the girls choose four boys from a suite just like their own. Through their letters, the girls learn a lot about their new pen pals—and about themselves.

PEN PALS #2: TOO CUTE FOR WORDS

Palmer, the rich girl from Florida, has never been one for playing by the rules. So when she wants Amy's pen pal, Simmie, instead of her own, she simply takes him. She writes to Simmie secretly, and soon he stops writing to Amy. When Shanon, Lisa, and Amy find out why, the suite is in an uproar. How could Palmer be so deceitful? Before long, Palmer is thinking of leaving the suite—and the other girls aren't about to stop her. Where will it all end?

PEN PALS #3: P.S. FORGET IT!

Palmer is out to prove that her pen pal is the best—and her suitemate Lisa's is a jerk. When Lisa receives strange letters and a mysterious prank gift, it looks as if Palmer may be right. But does she have to be so smug about it? Soon it's all-out war in Suite 3-D!

From the sidelines, Shanon and Amy think something fishy is going on. Is the pen pal scheme going too far? Will it stop before Lisa does something she may regret? Or will the girls learn to settle their differences?

PEN PALS #4: NO CREEPS NEED APPLY

Palmer takes up tennis so she can play in the Alma-Ardsley tennis tournament with her pen pal, Simmie Randolph III. Lisa helps coach Palmer, and soon Palmer has come so far that they are both proud of her. But when Palmer finds herself playing *against*—not *with*—her super-competitive pen pal, she realizes that winning the game could mean losing *him*!

Palmer wants to play her best, and her suitemates will think she's a real creep if she lets down the school. Is any boy worth the loss of her friends?

PEN PALS #5: SAM THE SHAM

Palmer has a new pen pal. His name is Sam O'Leary, and he seems absolutely perfect! Palmer is walking on air. She can't think or talk about anything but Sam—even when she's supposed to be tutoring Gabby, a third-grader from town, as part of the school's community-service requirement. Palmer thinks it's a drag, until she realizes just how much she means to little Gabby. And just in time, too—she needs something to distract her from her own problems when it appears that there *is* no Sam O'Leary at Ardsley. But if that's the truth—who *has* been writing to Palmer?